Here Lies
the Librarian

ANNE
CUDDY

Here Lies
the Librarian

RICHARD PECK

SCHOLASTIC INC.

New York Toronto London Auckland Sydney
Mexico City New Delhi Hong Kong Buenos Aires

ISBN-13: 978-0-439-89885-0
ISBN-10: 0-439-89885-4

12 11 10 9 8 7 6 5 4 3 2   7 8 9 10 11 12/0

Printed in the U.S.A.   40

First Scholastic paperback printing, October 2007

Text set in Goudy

This book is dedicated to
Living librarians everywhere
And to my Dean
Beth Mehalick Paskoff

Here Lies
the Librarian

PART ONE

An Ill Wind

CHAPTER ONE
Twister in the Graveyard

I was cleaning carbon off a set of spark plugs with an emery cloth when my big brother Jake barged in, soaked to the skin.

"Twister," he said, "down around Roachdale." So we'd need to be underground before it got up by North Salem. Luckily it was broad daylight, so you could see this particular tornado coming. What we didn't know was that it was going to tear up the graveyard.

Just in case I dawdled, Jake took my arm in his big grip and ran me outside. This shed was the last place you'd want to be. In fact, it could be the last place you ever were. It was dirt-floored, without a cellar. A rickety canopy hung from the front, propped by two posts. A light summer breeze could lay the whole place flat.

1

It had started life as a livery stable. With hope in our hearts, we were calling it a garage now. We'd made an up-to-date sign to hang outside:

JAKE & PEEWEE'S GARAGE

GET	FLATS
GAS	FIXED

FREE AIR

It was flapping in the wind now, and so were we. Jake and I lit up through the grape arbor across old Colonel Hazelrigg's property. His storm cellar was around back where the land slopes up. It was a stout oak door set at a slant into a mound of earth.

The wind bent us double, and I lost my cap. It took all Jake's muscle to pull the door open. The wind squealed like pigs to the slaughter. "Get in there, Peewee," he yelled in my ear. "I'll go for the Colonel."

Colonel Hazelrigg was as apt to take shelter in his out-house as underground. I scuttled down stone steps, and the door dropped to above me. At first it was dark as a grave. But there were chinks enough to see, though without my cap, my hair was in my eyes.

It came to me that I wasn't alone. Over in the corner was what looked like a furry, toothy creature of field or ditch.

I squinted, and it was Aunt Hat Hazelrigg. She squinted back. As she was plastered from stem to stern with feathers from her Rhode Island Reds, the tornado must have caught her trying to chase her chickens into the brooder house. I marveled that a woman that ancient and puny could lift the storm cellar door by herself. But she had an arm on her. She slumped in silence, a woman of few words.

The storm cellar doubled as cold storage. It's where you kept your apples and onions and potatoes through the winter, and anything you'd put up. Aunt Hat hunched under a shelf of glass jars webbed together, gray pickled pigs' feet.

The rain hammered the door above us and found all the chinks. I was blinder than a mole when the door jerked open and Jake threw in Sparks. He was a hound dog that hung around the garage. Though he wasn't quite ours, he wasn't anybody else's either. We called him Sparks. I don't know what his name was. He hit hard, and his tongue dealt me a glancing blow.

Colonel Hazelrigg stumbled in next, handed down by Jake, with water running off both of them. The Colonel sagged against me. Looked like he was wearing his Romeo bedroom slippers. Luck was with us because he had his pants on. Jake followed, and when the door dropped down again, it was a full house.

We hunkered on the wet stones, our knees intermingling. Sparks shook a gallon of rainwater over us. Colonel Hazelrigg fought for breath. But he rallied. "Keep your heads down, boys," he said. "Them Rebs can see around corners. And for the sake of the girls and women you left behind, keep your powder dry."

The Colonel could be clear in his mind, sometimes for long stretches. But any quick change, anything sudden, and he was back fighting the Civil War.

The wind roared like a freight train, and Sparks clawed the floor, trying to get lower. Then came that awful silence, and you could feel the air being drawn out of your lungs. The light through the chinks was sulfur yellow. We were in the eye of the storm. "Boys," the Colonel said, "let us pray."

You lose track of time, but by and by the wind came round again. The rain drove in waves, punishing the door. Every time a big limb struck it, we rattled around like a box of loose parts.

A while longer, and the wind began to whine down. You could get your breath back. "Never trust the quiet," the Colonel warned. "Be not deceived. They's a sharpshooter in every tree, a skirmisher back of every bush. One of them bullets could be engraved with your name."

Aunt Hat sighed.

When we couldn't even hear a spatter of rain, Jake shouldered the door open, and it fell back. Black clouds boiled above us. Sparks leaped out and charged off in every direction. It appeared to be night to him, and he was looking for a moon to bay at.

Jake pulled the Colonel out, and I followed. Between us we set Aunt Hat on her pins.

She looked around. Not a windowpane of their sloping old house was cracked. But the big lilac bush beside it was nothing but naked twigs now, rising from a drift of purple snow. The grape arbor was pretty much down to tendrils.

The Colonel's bold nose consulted the wind, and his old eyes blazed. Leaves whipped out of his white hair. He was a sight, but seemed to think the Rebels were in full retreat. Aunt Hat had on the Civil War forage cap she wore for a gardening hat. Her skirts were tucked up in a web belt also from the war. She wandered off to count her chickens.

Down by the road, the garage still stood, even the canopy. Our house next door, Jake's and mine, survived, though with fewer shingles.

The Colonel turned on us and seemed to sheathe his sword, but he was naturally not allowed anything sharp. Though a dead ringer for General Robert E. Lee, he was fighting on the other side. "All present and accounted for?"

We were, so Jake thought we'd head uptown to see the damage there. The air was still full of stuff.

"Strike the tents," the Colonel commanded, and we headed out.

We all lived on the outskirts, way out in the weeds. Between us and town was the Beulahland cemetery. The road was a mess, every hoofprint brimming with rainwater. Out in the ruts, we saw trouble. A shade tree out of the middle of the graveyard was crossways in the ditch. Great big tree with the loose dirt blowing off its roots.

A bald buzzard thudded down in the field opposite. It was the spitting image of old Judge Ransom. Jake muttered something and broke into a lope, though when you think about it, there was no real hurry.

A woven-wire fence enclosed the cemetery. That's as far as Sparks went. The fur rose all down his backbone, and he whined and talked to himself and edged backwards.

I wasn't overjoyed myself. We went in by the gate, and all the pathways were blocked with wet brush. We knew a good many of the residents, though the oldest part went back to the 1830s. I looked for Othmar Gunderson, though he was before my time:

OTHMAR GUNDERSON

1844–1897

LATE TEACHER OF HOOSIER GROVE SCHOOL

STRUCK BY LIGHTNING WHILE

RETURNING FROM THE SCHOOL OUTHOUSE

"AH SWEET MYSTERY OF LIFE"

And would you believe it? There was my cap right there on top of the Gunderson gravestone, like the tornado had gently placed it there.

I grabbed it and caught up with the Colonel and Jake, pushing through fallen limbs ahead of me. Jake looked back. "Peewee, this is about as far as you need to go."

The twister had skipped across the graveyard like a

stone across a pond. Every whipstitch you could see the earth turned up in big raw heaves. There was stuff in the trees too that ought not to be there. My heart was in my mouth. I looked past the Colonel and Jake and saw the tornado had opened a grave. The coffin was thrust up, and the lid of it elsewhere.

At least it wasn't Mama. I was sure of that. Mama was buried under a willow over by an open field. So of course, like a fool, I had to take a look.

The coffin was half out of the ground at a sharp angle. It had a mahogany finish. The metal label screwed to it read:

EVERY WOOD PART GUARANTEED STOVE-DRIED

APEX CABINETRY & COFFINS

BEANBLOSSOM, INDIANA

ALL WORK TO YOUR SPECIFICATIONS

NEVER A COMPLAINT

The Colonel was examining the coffin's contents. He pulled on his beard, and I supposed he thought he was at Gettysburg. But I was wrong.

"Why, looky there, if that ain't Gladys Poundstone, Gladys Gilmore as was. I took her to the victory ball the Republicans give when U.S. Grant was elected in eighteen hundred and sixty-eight. Howdy, Gladys!"

Jake was looking around for the lid. I peered past him into the coffin. Being fourteen, I often acted before I thought.

What I noticed first was that Gladys Gilmore Poundstone's hair had kept growing, long after death. It flowed a yellowed white from her gray skull down to cover most of her face, mercifully. Across her sunken bosom her hands were clasped, and there was precious little flesh on them. Her fingernails had kept on growing too. You don't want to know how long. Her dress was several stained shades of green and long out of style now. I was thinking about being sick.

"Well, dog my cats, Gladys." Colonel Hazelrigg shook his old head. "Imagine you turning up after all this time."

Jake found the lid and brought it back. It had screwed down, but the screws were sheared. Never mind, he and I both had pockets full of nails. I always kept the ones I found in punctured inner tubes. Jake was never without a claw-hammer on his belt loop. He was building an automobile of his own design from parts, so he was a walking tool chest.

I breathed easier after we got the lid back on. Without shovels, we couldn't bury it again, but we could make the lid tight against critters until the grave diggers could get out here.

I turned to go over and check on Mama, just to be sure. "Peewee, don't go that way," Jake said with a nail in his mouth. "Go around."

But why go around? Anywhere you turned was skinned bark and brush up to your—

Then I saw. There was something up a tree between here and Mama. I wanted it to be a wad of old rags. But if it was, they were wearing boots.

Still, I wanted it to be anything but what it was. A scarecrow, maybe. It wasn't. It was a skeleton in the rotten rags of a dress suit and boots. The boots had wooden soles, so he dated back a ways. The tornado had dug him up, blown him out of his box, and wedged him in the high crotch of a Dutch elm. From his raggedy coat sleeves, finger bones hung down. I gagged.

"I can't call him by name offhand," the Colonel remarked. "But he belonged to the Masonic lodge. You can see his apron from here." I wretched.

By now I was crashing through the undergrowth, making for Mama. I was nearly there when something soft and damp slapped my face. I reined in and pulled back. It was a sickening pink, with fringe, blanket-sized and snagged to two trees, like laundry on the line.

It was a shroud, shell pink. The tornado had dug up some other coffin, unwound this shroud from somebody— some body—and flung it for these trees to catch.

I whimpered and darted forth, head low. Now I was crazy to know if Mama was undisturbed. At last I'd picked my way to the fenceline where she was. A willow wept over her, and the headstone was untouched:

MCGRATH

ALVAH HICKENLOOPER

1869–1907

CALLED BACK

I dropped down to clear away the brush. Sheltered beneath was a cluster of white violets, abloom. I'd planted them one time when I was visiting her. She'd been gone half my life, and I couldn't quite recall her like I wanted to. Now I only remembered remembering her.

Papa wasn't with her, or anywhere near. He'd never been able to settle down after Mama died. In the end, he drifted down to Mexico, hoping to hook up with Pancho Villa. When he got in the way of a firing squad, they buried him where he fell.

As I turned away from Mama, I noticed Miss Dietz's grave, over there by a sticker bush. The wind had spared her too. She'd been the town librarian, back when we had one. Her stone read:

ELECTRA DIETZ

1851–1912

SHH

HERE LIES THE LIBRARIAN

AFTER YEARS OF SERVICE,

TRIED AND TRUE,

HEAVEN STAMPED HER——

OVERDUE

It was no surprise to me that the tornado had left her be. Nothing could stir Miss Dietz's stumps as much as coming after you for a book fine. We'd crossed swords once too often, and I'd been banned for life from the library at the age of ten.

When they found her checked out under the card catalog, the board of trustees took the opportunity to shut down the library.

It saved the township a six-hundred-and-fifty-dollar annual salary, and it was okay by me. As quick as I could get my school days behind me, I meant to be an auto mechanic at my brother's garage, and a good one. Nothing about the library had a thing to do with yours truly. That's what I thought. And being fourteen, I believed me.

CHAPTER TWO

A Fistful of Library Cards
in Her Cold Hand

It's an ill wind that doesn't blow somebody some good. The tornado that touched down on that spring day in 1914 blew Jake and me an entirely new fortune.

As tornados go, it broke no records, though it broke up a lot of other stuff. It didn't kill anybody, though, and gave a few of the already dead a good airing.

And me a bad night. Every time a branch scraped the windowpane, I'd bounce in the bed, sure it was the old skeleton in the dress suit come to get me. I was up and down the livelong night. Then bolt awake in the deepest reaches of it.

Any little thing could rouse me. From the day Jake and I went into business, we'd been plagued by vandals and pilferers. They'd knocked the padlock off the garage door more than once. And we'd lose handfuls of drill bits and anything handy. People said when the paved road came through, it would bring in a bad element of people. If you asked me, they'd been here all along.

A night breeze like heavy breathing stirred the feed sacks at my window. Moonlight—something—beckoned me to the sill. Outside, the world was black, edged in white. A bent figure moved across the property through the mist and murk, along the back way from Beulahland. This creature of the night came to an open patch drenched in moonlight.

It was Aunt Hat, heading home from the graveyard, in overalls. She never took them off, and wore them under her skirts in daylight. Draped over and around her was an exceptionally long shawl, fringed. White in the moonlight, but I knew it was shell pink.

I cringed fitfully in the bed till morning. Various fears rode me like a horse.

But the town itself got off pretty easy, considering. Mrs. B. D. Klinefelder's wash had been on the line, and the tornado distributed it all over town. Anybody rounding a gusty corner was subject to being smacked in the kisser by a pair of her massive step-ins. Mr. Klinefelder's truss snapped like a pennant from a pole for days. Small boys shot it to rags with air rifles and pump-action pellet guns until the telephone people came out to haul it down.

Though the old library building stood abandoned, the storm broke out the front window. But the only book known to escape was *Tales From the New Testament Retold for the Littlest Christians*. It sailed down the street to knock the sign off the pool hall. Certain local elements said it was the Hand of Providence.

The hotel lost its roof, but it was hurting for business anyway. Traveling salesmen—drummers—used to come in by train, hire a horse and trap from the Colonel, and put up at the hotel. But now the drummers were braving the roads to come by motorcar and were gone again by dark. They'd paved the Indianapolis road as near us as Brownsburg, and we were looking for slab by fall.

The Colonel called automobiles "devil wagons" for what they'd done to his business. But the old livery stable made a dandy garage for Jake and me. They couldn't pave in front of us quick enough. But as long as the dirt road kept turning up horseshoe nails, we had flats to fix. We'd had us a pretty fair winter. It was the first one people didn't put their autos up on blocks and go back to the horse.

Still, it seemed to me that Jake's dreams were bigger than a garage by the side of the road. He was my brother. I could hear him dreaming.

We kept reasonably busy that Saturday after the tornado. Farmers came in to gawk at the damage, many in wagons. But Jake wasn't too proud to repair a whiffletree.

Betweentimes, he worked in the back stall, building his own automobile from the axles up. He'd come by a little old Leland-Faulconer engine out of an Oldsmobile runabout. By strict precision in his machining, he was going to get ten horses out of that little three-horsepower engine by August or know why not. He was an artist with a file.

He'd have me turn the crank slow to test how fat the spark was. With our heads close, we'd listen to that sizzle of electricity as it popped in one plug after another. I'd never driven an auto—didn't know how—but I knew the feel of an engine warm and alive under my hand, throbbing like a heart.

Round about then, we heard an automobile plowing a furrow down the road, which was like a slop jar with all the recent rains. I glanced out of the shed just as the auto swayed around the fallen tree outside Beulahland cemetery.

It was a little Stoddard-Dayton, fitted with a close-coupled body. That meant seats for two in front and another two behind. All four were filled, and the automobileer was a female.

Women were driving, now that Cadillac had introduced the electric self-starter. You didn't have to squat down in the mud to crank an engine alive, which was hard to do in corsets and a big hat. Besides, it could break your arm. The Cadillac slogan,

Crank from your seat,
Not from the street,

put women behind the wheel and on the open road. You'd even get farm women at the wheels of Model T's, coming to town to trade eggs for snuff.

The Stoddard-Dayton found the right ruts and rode them forward. The three passengers were female too— khaki canvas hats and veils.

As they drew even with us, Sparks pounded out on the road. Though he thought he owned the garage, he hated an automobile worse than the Colonel did. He was barking his brains out and trying to bite a wheel, which unnerved the driver.

She wrenched the auto out of the ruts. It swung this way and blew a tire. I jumped back. Small shrieks came from the other three females, but the driver just thumped the steering wheel with the heel of her gloved hand. "How provoking," she said, or "botheration," or words to that effect.

Realizing he'd gone too far this time, Sparks disappeared into weeds.

Though the others twittered among themselves, the pilot climbed down. Her skirts were hobbled, being the latest thing, so it took her some time. She wore washable driving togs, but they'd never been outside Indianapolis.

"I suppose we can count ourselves lucky that this happened in front of a garage," she informed the others. When she threw back her veil, I saw she was only nineteen or twenty—Jake's age. She reached into her bosom and drew out spectacles on a chain—pince-nez, they were called. They fitted onto the bridge of her nose.

She gave me the once-over. Sadly, this was not the first day for my overalls or the shirt under it. And there'd be a given amount of grease on my face and ears. "Was that your dog?" she inquired.

"No, ma'am! Never seen him before." I didn't want her to think we sicced a dog on traffic to get business. Some garage owners—naming no names—were known to strew the road with nails to improve their tire patch trade.

"We were looking for a place to picnic anyway," the young lady said. "Someplace dry underfoot?"

"If you don't mind ragweed," I said, "there's a grape arbor back up behind, with a table in it."

They were spattered anyway and wore elk-skin boots, probably knee-high.

Barring the spectacles that made her severe, she was a really good-looking girl. She had skin on her like a peach.

Jake was working over his hands with a dirty rag. Their eyes seemed to meet, and he looked pole-axed as I'd never seen him.

The young lady said to him, "Could you patch the tire while we lunch?"

"Peewee can do it," Jake rumbled. He was somewhat gun-shy of the opposite sex. He may also have been the best-looking boy in Hendricks County, and probably Boone.

"We've motored out from the city to see the tornado damage," she said to him.

"Ah," Jake said, receding to the back stalls of the garage, but no farther than his workbench.

She watched him recede. Finally, I said, "The arbor's around back. And if you need to, you can use the out—"

"Thank you so much," she blurted, and called, "Girls, to the arbor!" The others were unroping a hamper from the back of the Stoddard-Dayton, atwitter still. Off they went, twittering and tittering and teetering behind their leader.

In their absence, I set to, getting the rim off the wheel, the tire off the rim, and the tube out of the tire. It was a Kelly-Springfield. Then I went to work to locate the leak. I pumped up the tube till I heard the snake-hiss of air escaping and found the place.

By this time, the young lady was back. She'd settled the others up in the arbor, and come back, drawn to the garage. Maybe she wanted to see if I really knew how to patch a tube. Maybe not.

"Quite a peculiar old gentleman appeared to us up in the arbor," she said. "He seemed to think we were Civil War nurses."

"That'd be the Colonel. It's his arbor." I looked up from my labors. "Did he try to run you off?"

"Not when I told him I was Clara Barton," the young lady said.

That was quick thinking. She looked on while I scraped the tube around the hole with sandpaper and squeezed a dab of rubber cement over the spot.

"But my name is, in fact, Irene Ridpath." She spoke in a voice full enough to bounce off the back wall of the garage.

As she seemed to be speaking to me, I said, "Are them other girls your sisters?"

"Grace, Lodelia, and Geraldine?" she said. "They are my sorority sisters."

"Oh," I said, not knowing. "Are they silly?"

"Somewhat silly," Irene Ridpath replied, "but they will settle. We are co-educational students at Butler University, in the Library Science course."

"Oh," I said.

"I see the local library here is boarded up."

Now I was cutting a patch of raw rubber and clamping the deflated tube on a vise.

"And Miss Dietz, the librarian, is in Beulahland," I said, intent on my work.

"Beulahland?" Miss Ridpath said. "Oh, you mean:

"LOOK ROUND! IN ORDERLY ARRAY

SEE WHERE THE BURIED HOST AWAIT THE

JUDGMENT DAY."

These were the words spelled out over the graveyard gate.

"That's the place," I said. "They found her, dead though on duty, with a fistful of library cards in her cold hand."

"Ah," Irene said. "Expired."

All this time, nothing save silence came from the back of the garage.

"And you are . . . ?" Miss Ridpath chanced.

"We're the McGraths. Jake there, he's my brother."

He was shier by the minute, scarcely a shadow on the rear wall now. We'd left up all the old tin signs from livery stable days: the ads for patent horse remedies, and the blackboard to keep track of horses hired out. A notice remained from the Colonel's time:

WHIP LIGHT
DRIVE SLOW
PAY CASH
BEFORE YOU GO

The only new sign was a poster for this summer's Hendricks County fair, announcing its stock auto race and picturing the dirt track.

I touched a match to a little can of fuel under the vise. In a couple minutes the tube would be patched and vulcanized.

"You're masterful at that . . . Peewee," Irene Ridpath said in a complimentary way.

"But not cheap," I said. "This will run you fifty cents.

It'd be seventy-five in Indianapolis," added I who'd never been there.

"And you'll need you gas to get you back there," I said, businesslike, "and I better have a look at your grease cups. Let's call it a dollar even."

If you cooked the patch too long, the rubber cracked, and the patch worked loose. I took it off the heat, checked the valve, and bent to pump up the tube.

That's when events veered off in a new direction. I went to work, pumping. As the tube began to find its shape, I reached up to wipe away the sweat of my brow. By chance, the cap I wore fell off, and my mass of hair fell out, flowing red as lava down my back.

Irene Ridpath jumped back against a display of Shaler Portable Vulcanizers. Her feet danced for purchase on the greasy dirt floor.

"But you're a girl!" She grasped at her throat. Her pince-nez swung from the chain. "Who *are* you??"

"Eleanor," I said, "but I hate the name. Eleanor McGrath."

"But you're not a boy!" Irene was whiter than chalk.

"I never said I was."

CHAPTER THREE
Alone by the Boneyard Gate

"I blame myself," Jake said at supper. Dusk crept across our kitchen table. He was outlined against the dying day. "I've let things go on way too long. You're gettin' too old to be . . . like you are. People don't know whether you're a—"

"If you're speaking to me," I said, pert, "I don't know what you're talking about. Besides, what people? School people don't count. And we don't know anybody else, except to speak to. Except the Hazelriggs, and nobody can figure out what Aunt Hat is either."

Jake raked a square hand through his curly hair. His curled. Mine kinked.

In my heart, I blamed Irene Ridpath for this. One look at her and Jake had decided he'd been letting me run wild.

He was all turned around in his mind and taking it out on me. As if I could be Irene Ridpath, in a million years.

"Besides, who took me coon hunting?" I said, scratching up under my shirt. "Who was it took me to the crick to fish?" I let him remember the nights we'd treed a coon by lantern light. And that hour of evening when the bass jumps out of the water for bugs, and there we are with our dip nets. And our duck blind, on the sandbank, in the fall of the year with the geese veeing overhead. I let him remember.

He sighed. He'd been sighing ever since he met Irene Ridpath, though only to himself. "Look at you," he said. "You're gettin' . . . bigger. Before we know it, you'll be busting out of one of my shirts."

My face went hot. "Watch your mouth."

"I'm just sayin'," he said, kind of discouraged.

"I've got a dress. I wear it to school, don't I? I got Mama's things. But I'm sure as shoot not going to wear a durn dress to patch a tire or take a cylinder head apart."

"And that's another problem," Jake mumbled.

"What?"

"I said you could use you a new dress for your eighth-grade graduation."

"If I go," I muttered.

"And you'll be needing new duds—girls' duds—when you go to town for high school," Jake said, "come fall."

"Do they teach automobile mechanics at the high school?" I inquired.

"Not to girls, which is what you—"

"Then I ain't going," I said.

"You'll be taking Home Economics and Cookery and such as that, which wouldn't hurt you."

"I said I ain't going."

"And grammar," Jake remarked.

"High school did very little for yours," I said. "Anyhow, I wouldn't know anybody. Who'll be going in to the high school from Hoosier Grove School, for Pete's sake?"

"You can help out around the garage in the afternoons after high school lets out," Jake offered, "when you don't have homework."

"We'll see," I said.

"You'll go," he said.

At least we were eating good that night. I was no hand to cook, and neither was Jake. We could just about get by on hoecakes and clabber. But some evenings we'd find better eats left on the porch. They were from Aunt Hat, who couldn't stand to be thanked. Tonight we had a pan of her cornbread baked with bacon. We crumbled it into sweet milk and made a meal out of it.

"And don't eat with your elbows on the table," Jake said.

"Your elbows are on the table," I said.

"You're a girl," he said.

As quick as we finished, Jake made his escape. He took a lamp and went back down to the garage to work on his automobile. It needed to be ready and rolling by county fair time. Besides, he was easier in his mind with machinery than with me.

I had to light a lamp myself, to do the dishes, which got the grease out of my hands, most of it. In the dark window over the sink appeared the ghost of my reflection. The fiery red of my tangled mane was dimmed by dark, so it wasn't quite me. My eyes were two smudges, but I could make out my mouth.

"How provoking," I said, to see the shape of the words reflected. "Botheration."

Making my mouth pear-shaped to match my tones, I said, "Quite a peculiar old gentleman appeared to us up in the arbor."

I wished I could talk like that, but who'd believe it, coming from me?

" 'Look round,' " I told the window, " 'in orderly array. See where the buried host await the Judgment Day,' " while down in the garage, Jake's thoughts were all on Irene Ridpath too. I know. I can hear him dreaming.

I let him dream on, as I had some private business to conduct that particular evening. It would be a lead-pipe cinch to slip off the property since Jake was in his private world down at the garage. And who knew when I'd get back? If everything worked to plan, I'd very likely spend the rest of the night in the Hendricks County jail. If I'd owned a toothbrush, I'd have brought it along.

The situation was this: Eighth-grade graduation was next week. Steps had to be taken, or I'd end up having to attend the ceremony itself. This I had no intention of doing in my old dress or a new one.

I had no intention in this world of sitting through Wilma Boggs's piano rendition of "Silver Threads Among the Gold." Nor the choral rendition of "I'm a Yankee Doodle Dandy." But I especially had no intention of speaking a piece, as all graduates were forced to do, on a platform.

So I meant to get myself arrested that night, reasoning that it would bar me from graduation exercises. Finishing out the school year itself was torment enough for anybody.

As Jake and I lived out in the county, we'd had to go to an old-timey one-room schoolhouse the other way from town. I hadn't minded at first when Jake still went there too. But he was long graduated, and I was ready.

Hoosier Grove was the poorest excuse for a place of learning you can think of. Three or four of us in each grade and scarcely a brain among us. A library of four books propped on the windowsill. The teacher was Miss Daisy Daggett, a dried-up old shrew and very quick with her ruler on your knuckles.

Being an eighth-grader of the oldest class cut no ice with me, as I was always more interested in older kids than anybody my age. So I didn't give two hoots about anybody there.

Still, four of us were graduating that particular spring and I made sure to befriend two of them. The third was a girl, Wilma Boggs, and therefore useless to my plan.

But I managed to fall in with the two boys, Elwood Soper and Crandall Boggs, a cousin to Wilma. Practically everybody was cousins at Hoosier Grove.

Anyway, being boys, Elwood and Crandall had no more interest in attending the graduation exercises than I did myself. Still, I had to talk them around, and they were slow in their thinking. Crandall Boggs had sucked his thumb till after Christmas of sixth grade. Elwood Soper was eternally digging stuff out of his ears with a twig. But they were boys, and even a chance of spending overnight in jail appealed to them both. Though I'd had to plant the idea in their thick heads and sweeten the deal with some horehound candy.

I stole off our place into the night, along the back way to Beulahland cemetery to meet up with Elwood and Crandall as planned. Over my shoulder was slung a gunny sack with several rocks of the right size and a big rusty pair of tail-and-mane scissors left over from the livery-stable days.

The night was dark as pitch, but I found my way. Boys would sooner meet at a graveyard gate than anywhere else.

Though the hoot of an owl made my rocks rattle, I thought it was a nice touch to such a night as this.

I crept around the outside of the graveyard, keeping the woven-wire fence in reach. But I planned to tell my classmates that I'd walked bravely through Beulahland, stepping on graves, if I got to the gate before them.

I seemed to. All was lonesome emptiness at the graveyard gate.

It was chillier than I'd figured, still springtime, with a breeze carrying odd sounds from the direction of the grave stones. I thought of a certain tree, a Dutch elm, with something up in its crotch. I recalled Gladys Gilmore Poundstone, back in the ground with any luck.

It was damp out here too. Nothing had dried out since the tornado. My flesh felt like the moss in a bait can.

As the quiet began to move in on me, thundering in my ears, I whistled small tunes, anything I could remember except "I'm a Yankee Doodle Dandy." My teeth chattered, but I kept my eyes peeled, though you could barely see a cow's length ahead.

It crossed my mind that Elwood and Crandall, being boys, were planning to sneak up on my blind side to scare the living—

A branch snapped inside the black graveyard. Of course it could be Aunt Hat on one of her errands. But I shivered and shrank. Silence followed, though I strained to hear more. But then what sound would a single hand make, clawing out of a loamy grave? A hand with fingernails still growing.

I was turning to cold stone out here, and with nowhere halfway dry to sit but my sack of rocks and that pointy pair of horse scissors. Where were Elwood and Crandall, my confederates? Had them little owlhoots bypassed me? Were they already uptown, moving up on the hitching rail outside the pool hall? Did they take my plan and run off with it, leaving me alone by the boneyard gate, scareder than I'd care to mention?

It was so quiet now you could hear the clock striking from the bell tower all the way uptown. It might have been ten but could be eleven. Now every branch on a graveyard tree was reaching for me. Did I want to be in this particular place when midnight struck?

My mind turned toward home, and my warm bed beckoned. Why it didn't occur to me to take off for town by myself I couldn't tell you. Maybe I didn't like the idea of being locked up alone overnight in a cell without the boys. Home was calling me now at the top of its lungs.

I wouldn't need my rocks, but I carried the horse scissors home. They might be missed, and I'd be armed on the way. It was closer by road, but I moseyed on up the back way. When Beulahland was behind me, I breathed better, but I was no easier in my mind. Whether Elwood and

Crandall were at home, tucked up in their ticks, sound asleep, or whether they were uptown trying to get within reach of the long arm of the law hardly mattered.

What they'd done was leave me high but not dry at the graveyard gate.

What they'd done was—treat me like a girl.

I naturally plotted revenge. I pictured in my mind blood splattering from their noses laid flat across their faces. I saw their already oversized ears swollen from a good boxing. I heard them sucking for air while I held them under the water of the horse trough with my firm fists on their necks. Being a girl, I was bigger than both of them.

But these satisfying thoughts seeped away. As recently as last week, I'd have carried out an awful vengeance. But now everything was different somehow. Now I knew the next time I saw them weedy little polecats, I'd look right over their heads. I'd switch my skirttails past them on the way to my desk. I'd be too womanly to lower myself down to their level.

Again, I blamed Irene Ridpath and that brief moment when she'd crossed our lives, Jake's and mine. Even going to jail didn't seem like much fun now. It seemed kind of backwoodsy and lowdown. And childish.

Back on our property, I noticed that garage and house were silent and unlit. I crept up the porch stairs, avoiding the creaky part. I was *this close* to our front door when a ton of bricks hit me from behind. Down I went, sprawled on the porch floor, my nose rooting up splinters. The horse scissors skidded away. I shrieked like a scalded cat. Or a girl.

Something, somebody, was all over me. "Get off and turn me—"

"Peewee?" Jake let up on me and grabbed me by the scruff of the neck. "Peewee, dadburn it! What in the—"

He'd thought I was one of them vandals who come to turn over our property and steal our stuff around this time of night. "Why aren't you up in bed? What in the Sam Hill come over you?"

By evil chance, he'd just locked up the garage and was making his way up the yard as I'd come home. The only luck I seemed to have was bad.

"You're getting more like Aunt Hat right along." He gave me a good shake. "What did you think you were doing out here in the dark? And what are them? The horse shears? What are you up to? And try the truth."

I had to tell him. Spitting out paint chips, I recounted the whole dumb plan from start to this finish. I explained how me and Elwood and Crandall planned to get ourselves thrown in the pokey so we'd be too shamed to attend graduation exercises.

"How?" Jake said.

"Well," I said, glad for the dark, "I had a sack of rocks, and me and Elwood and Crandall—"

"Never mind about them," Jake said.

"We were going to put rocks under the saddles of the horses tied up outside the pool hall."

This was an old stunt, so old it had whiskers on it. You put rocks under a saddle, and when the rider mounted up, the rocks dug in and the horse bucked. And maybe threw him in the trough. Also, of course, anybody coming out of the pool hall was apt to be half drunk at least, though it was a dry county.

Jake sighed. "And don't tell me," he said. "You were going to crop the horses' tails and manes with the scissors."

"And get caught doing it," I mumbled, "so I wouldn't have to—"

"You'll be going to graduation exercises," Jake said, real strict. "Make your mind up to that."

And so I went, though I can't bear to recall the actual exercises in any detail. I even had a new dress for the occasion, new to me. I found it out on the porch, tied up in butcher paper, on graduation morning. It was from Aunt Hat, and I can only hope it came from her closet and not off a corpse. It was blue-and-red-striped sateen with a bombazine bodice, and she'd done her best to cut it to fit me. There was loose material behind that might have contained a bustle.

But I wore it, just that one time, and Wilma Boggs didn't look that much better in a new dress with knife pleats.

And I had to give my piece too, speaking right up. We were all to make speeches concerning Famous People of the Past. Wilma went on at length about Jenny Lind, the Swedish Nightingale. Elwood told us about Benjamin Franklin, the discoverer of electricity, and Crandall droned on about Eli Whitney and his cotton gin.

I'd looked around for somebody who hadn't lived that long and came up with Nancy Hanks Lincoln (1784–1818), who was the mother of Honest Abe and died right here in Indiana of the milk sickness, having drunk milk from a cow that ate white snakeroot. The end.

Anyway, I graduated, and that was all the school I wanted, and let's say no more about it.

CHAPTER FOUR

The Peerless, the Packard, the Pierce-Arrow

The tornado of 1914 blew us very little more business. Even the off-chance of glimpsing a well-dressed skeleton in a tree crotch lost its draw.

We'd hoped for more out-of-town traffic. We never got much trade from the locals. Uptown, Kirbys' MotorKar Kare garage hogged the business and serviced all the best people. We took leavings and looked down the road, hoping for pavement.

But the twister created another tempest. Our local newspaper was mostly advertisements for sheep dip, hen grit, and cures for female complaints. Most people read the Brownsburg paper. It was a nearby town, bigger than us, and stuck up with very little reason.

Whenever the Brownsburg Bugle bothered to cover our news, they called us "Rubesburg." An article appeared that next Tuesday under "Regional Notes From Our Outlying Communities":

RUBESBURG LIBRARY REPAIRS PERMANENTLY SHELVED

Last week's tornado that extensively remodeled our neighboring village's hotel and unearthed several old settlers broke out the window of the long-defunct public library. This structure at the heart of "town" will be recalled by older readers as the former Proctor & Thayer Feeds and Grains.

Librarian Miss Electra Dietz, the former Cerberus and Gorgon of that particular repository of world civilization, met her Maker better than two years ago.

Evidently the Rubesburg "city" fathers have nary a plan to replace either windowpane or librarian. But then, if you could read, what would you be doing in Rubesburg?

Only rude scorn from Brownsburg could have moved our library board. They called themselves to order and hired Claude Fenster, the glazier, to replace the library's front window, forty-eight dollars from the public coffers, installed.

More hue and cry followed about hiring a new librarian to replace Miss Dietz. Older residents said that kind of money would be better spent rebuilding the hitching rails and horse troughs along the main street. It was, at this time before the hard road, a backward-looking place.

These events passed Jake and me by. We lived out on the Crawfordsville road in a straggle of houses and that many privies called Hazelrigg Settlement, named for the Colonel, our only landmark. We were bigger rubes than Rubesburg.

But one morning the mailman stopped—Wendell Mickelmass, still horse-drawn. I was digging us a grease pit beside the garage. Uptown, Kirbys' MotorKar Kare had a hydraulic lift so they could work under autos and even limousines and hearses. Not expecting to see our own hydraulic lift in this lifetime, I was digging a grease pit, axle-wide and about ten foot long.

"Hey, Peewee," Wendell Micklemass called over, "digging your own grave?" Which was his level of humor. In the Colonel's day, a bunch of men hung out at the livery stable to loaf and tell lies. They called themselves the "Spit-n-Whittle Club." I think Wendell missed it. He went on in the garage to bother Jake.

I heard him say, "Anybody named 'Miss Eleanor McGrath' kin to you'ens?"

"That'd be Peewee," Jake said.

I liked to keel over. I'd never had a letter, and my hands were filthy.

Wendell swung out of the garage with a small envelope. "Letter for Miss Eleanor La-de-Dah Mc—"

"Give it here, Wendell." I stuck it down my overalls bib.

"Don't you want to see what it says?"

"After you're gone."

When Wendell went, I wiped my hands and drew forth an envelope of the palest lavender with a two-cent stamp, postmarked in Indianapolis. I'd never seen my real name spelled out in such loops and swoops. I hated to tear the envelope, but couldn't wait.

It was written from a Meridian Street address and read as follows:

> *My dear Eleanor,*
>
> *By rights, I should have written sooner, after the pleasure of meeting you and your brother. Indeed, I regret certain confusions that followed, hoping our encounter is not a painful memory to yourself.*

How ladylike, I marveled, reading on:

> *My reason for writing is that my sorority sisters and I are all determined to apply for the position of public librarian, advertised by your board of trustees.*
>
> *As the interviews are to be held at a public*

meeting, I hope both you and your brother
might be there as our only friends in the
community.
                 Yours for literacy and enlightenment,
                          (Miss) Irene Ridpath

I kept the letter, it being my first.

The day of the library board's public meeting came round at last. I was going to be there with bells on, though it wouldn't be like Jake to shut down the garage in business hours.

I was upstairs at the house, jerking my back hair into a bow and working into one of Mama's old skirts. I wondered if I could pin it up to hobble it and learned I couldn't. I had a white shirtwaist to go on top, fairly white. Imagine my mirth when from the bedroom window I saw Jake's head under the pump. Now he'd skinned off his shirt and was washing his entire upper region.

I grinned.

When it was time to head uptown, he fell in step beside me. It was a quarter mile of weedy roadside between here and there.

"One of these days," Jake said, "we'll have us our own automobile to go in."

"We'd be at the meeting now if we had one," I said.

"What meeting?" he said, all bewilderment.

"The library board at the Oddfellows Hall." I rolled my eyes.

"I'm bound for the auto supply for a dry cell battery," said Jake, "and we're running low on 3-in-1 oil. Is the library meeting today?"

I chuckled down my shirtwaist. He was heading uptown for supplies in Papa's suitcoat? In June? Shaved? *You big liar,* I thought. But I slipped my hand into his. We swung along together, shaking the dust of the Hazelrigg Settlement from our boots.

On the way, we were all but sideswiped by an auto running amok all over the road. It was a Maxwell with Mrs. Olive Sugg at the wheel. She too was making for town at her top speed, as she was on the library board. Mrs. Sugg had paid extra for bumpers on the Maxwell, fore and aft. A good investment because she ran into things. In her country drives she'd killed more chickens than a hotel kitchen.

Through Mrs. Sugg's dust, we saw uptown was thronged. Any outrage as big as hiring a librarian was bound to bring everybody out of the woodwork. The hitching rail was chock-a-block with horses and wagons and here and there a farmer's tin Lizzie, which is what the Ford Model T was called at that time. I didn't see Irene Ridpath's Stoddard-Dayton.

But a caravan of four automobiles was drawing up before Prevo's General Merchandise, the store downstairs from the Oddfellows Hall. We rarely saw such autos as these up close.

"By golly, that's a Stutz." Jake nearly broke into a trot. It was a tourer with a six-pane isinglass rear window above double spare tires. Behind it was a Peerless, closed with draw-down curtains at the windows. And then—

"A Packard," Jake breathed. "Sweet—"

"A salon brougham," I said. I'd only seen pictures.

And at the rear, a Pierce-Arrow, lacquered in burnished Brewster green, its brass fittings golden in sunlight.

These were the famed three P's, the finest automobiles made in America: the Peerless, the Packard, the Pierce-Arrow, plus the Stutz, which was Indianapolis-built. They seemed to shame the very dust they'd raised.

Crowds made circles around them as the gaitered chauffeurs stood down from their side and the footmen from the other. As one man, they opened the limousines' rear doors and handed down four young ladies.

The high feathers on their hats nodded above the crowds as they crossed the plank sidewalk to the Oddfellows entrance. They were Irene's sorority sisters with Irene in the lead. Behind them four heavy men stepped down from the autos. They wore creamy city suits and stiff straw hats. Pearls stood in their neckties. Their hands blazed with Masonic rings. The fathers.

"Irene's dad owns a Pierce-Arrow," I whispered to Jake. "That Stoddard-Dayton was just her own little runabout."

Jake nodded gravely.

The sun struck black fire on the patent-leather bills of the chauffeurs' caps as they shook out the lap robes. Footmen dusted down the coachwork.

The crowd could hardly tear their eyes away, but then we all charged up the Oddfellows stairs. Jake too, forgetting all about the chores that had brought him uptown.

CHAPTER FIVE
The Bargain of the Century

Funeral parlor fans battered the air of the Oddfellows Hall. When I say everybody was there, I mean it. Wendell Mickelmass, the mailman, a flock of Boggses, several hulking Kirbys of Kirbys' MotorKar Kare. The Fensters. Two or three concerned preachers and their congregations. Mrs. B. D. Klinefelder in a new washdress. Everybody. The Colonel and Aunt Hat were there. Jake and I found seats nearby them.

Most of the multitude were there in hope of entertainment. But there were grumblers and troublemakers at the back, holding up signs:

KEEP OUR YOUNGENS INNOCENT

and

THE LIBERY ONLY NEEDS 2 BOOKS:
1. THE OLD TESTIMENT
2. THE NEW TESTIMENT

and

LESS BOOKS AND MORE TROUGHS
PITY THE PORE HORSE
YOU CAIN'T RIDE A BOOK

spelled as above. I'd never been in a crowd this big. I felt like a grain of wheat in a box of rat droppings.

The library trustees were three, on the platform with a spare chair.

One of the trustees was Old Man (Hans) Unrath, a rich skinflint farmer, and a bachelor, which made him cranky. Another was Mrs. Olive Sugg, pulling off her driving gloves. The third was Judge Ransom.

Down front Irene and her sorority sisters sat with their fathers. The only local candidate for the librarian job sat at the far end. I seemed to know that drawn chicken neck beneath the faded hair like an untidy haystack, drooped over by a weary hat.

Yes, it was Miss Daisy Daggett, teacher at Hoosier Grove School. I'd had that old bat for all eight grades. My heart sank at the sight of her, and my knuckles throbbed where her hardwood ruler had come down on them time and time again. I'd hoped against hope never to be in the same room with her ever again.

The judge rapped for order. Mrs. Sugg boomed, "Miss Daggett, be good enough to come forth."

The trustees settled her into the spare chair. She wore rusty black, and her hat had been familiar to all for years. Her shoes buttoned up the side.

"Kindly state your name and present position, if any."

"Daisy Daggett," Miss Daggett said, "Miss. Grade-school teacher."

"Your age?"

"I was a year behind you in school, Olive. Work it out."

Mrs. Sugg twitched. "Miss Daggett, why are you applying for the position of public librarian?"

"Because the kids are driving me cuckoo. In school, you got to keep them. In a public library, you can throw out the little—"

"And what do you find so difficult about your students?" Mrs. Sugg wondered.

"Well, if we're talking about your grandson, Walker Sugg, he set fire to—"

"We weren't speaking of my grandson, Miss Daggett."

The room leaned forward, thinking Miss Daggett and Mrs. Sugg might come to blows. But Old Man Unrath put in his two cents' worth.

"Say, Miss Daggett," he said, fingering his crepey wattles, "we got right at two hundred and twenty-five volumes in the library. Where do you stand on getting more?"

"More?" Miss Daggett looked startled. "More books means more shelves, and lumber's sky-high now."

"They's something about that woman I like," Old Man Unrath muttered. Oh, he was tight.

"And on the subject of remuneration," Judge Ransom said, "would you be content with the six-hundred-dollar salary, per annum?" He wore an elk's tooth on a gold chain straining across his front.

"Six hundred?" Miss Daggett goggled. "Electra Dietz was getting six fifty. Where do you get off trying to—"

"Ah, but the late Miss Dietz had completed the Basic Cataloging course at Terre Haute." The judge spoke in a voice flowing with milk and honey. "Have you?"

Mrs. Sugg smirked, and Miss Daggett clutched her pocketbook. "Six hundred for twelve months' enslavement when I'm doing better than that for nine? Let me tell you just exactly what you can do with—"

"Thank you, Miss Daggett." Mrs. Sugg made a long mark across her notes.

The crowd wheezed with relief. Jake and I weren't the only ones anxious to move on to the real candidates. Here the first one came now, being settled in the hot seat. Apart from Irene, she was the prettiest, in a candy-box way. She wore a hat called a toque. It went way up, and the feather went higher. She dazzled the room with a smile. Men melted.

Mrs. Sugg drew herself up, and there was a lot of her to draw on. "Your name and—"

"Grace Stutz, Miss. Co-educational student of Library Science at Butler U." A pointed slipper peeped from the slit in her skirt. Every man's eyes were cast down, as in prayer.

Jake jerked. "Her name's Stutz? She was *riding* in a Stutz. She's got a V-8 water-cooled engine under her hood," meaning the auto, of course.

"Miss Stutz," Mrs. Sugg began, "why—"

"I'll take this one," Old Man Unrath broke in. "Say, girly, what you want to be a librarian for anyhow? And speak right up. I'm deaf in the one ear and can't hear anything out of the other one."

"Because I like, BECAUSE I LIKE CHILDREN," Grace Stutz bellowed in a refined way.

"Then why don't you get married and have you some?" Old Man Unrath looked around, pleased with himself. The back row cheered and shook their signs.

Judge Ransom intervened. "And the salary offered?" he asked.

Grace had a pretty way of thinking, with one gloved finger in a dimple. Calculating, she said, "It is to the penny the dress allowance my father gives me."

Men sighed. Women moaned.

The judge stared. "Per annum?"

"Yes." Grace Stutz nodded. "And every year too."

When she stepped down, it was to a round of applause from thorny male hands.

"Next?" Mrs. Sugg said, frazzled. "And I think we can take it for granted that all the forthcoming applicants are Library Science students at Butler University."

A striking figure rose next. She was the tallest of the sorority if not the prettiest, and her pinstriped skirt was handsomely hobbled. An entire bird wing rode her hat, a raven's. When she turned to sit, we saw she wore a necktie very like a man's, depending from a tall collar. She riveted the room by fixing a monocle in one of her eyes. If she'd been silly before, she was all business now.

"Lodelia Fulwider," she said. "Indianapolis."

"And your qualifications," Mrs. Sugg said, "are—"

"'Bibliography and Reference Sources,'" Lodelia said, "'Administration of Libraries,' and, naturally, 'Basic Cataloging and Classification.' I have not as yet made a selection of my courses for the pending semester."

This silenced the board, who hadn't seemed to know there were this many courses in Library Science.

"And you would be prepared—"

"I am trained for the Registration desk, the Circulation desk, the Information desk, the Periodical—"

"We only got the one desk," yelped Old Man Unrath.

"At present," Lodelia Fulwider responded. "But expansion is the way forward. 'Rubesburg' now need not be 'Rubesburg' forever."

Old Man Unrath fell back, and the room stirred, especially the back row. Was she some kind of suffragette? She looked it. Were we going to get a lecture on women and the vote next?

"What a convincing case you make for progress, Miss Fulwider," the judge flowed. "Alas, we're not made of money."

"You don't need to be." Lodelia fixed him with her monocle. "I've also had the course in 'Book and Binding Repair.' I expect some of your books could use it."

"You mean to say you can fix books?" Old Man Unrath rallied. "You don't just keep on wanting to buy more?"

Lodelia nodded. "And I'm a firm believer in celluloid protective book covers." Then she quoted:

> *"Between covers all our days we crowd;*
> *The blanket first, and last the shroud."*

Silence fell over us. The back row wondered if she was quoting Scripture. We'd never run up against anybody this intellectual. Neither, I might add, had Brownsburg. Lodelia Fulwider's interview lasted little longer because she'd seemed to scare the rest of the questions out of the trustees.

"Miss Geraldine Harrison." The fourth candidate spoke clearly, letting the Harrison name soak into us. This

Indiana family had already produced two Presidents of the United States.

She was a big, rosy-cheeked young woman who'd have looked fine sitting a horse in less modern times than these. Nobody local had ever seen such an expensive hat. And confidence? She was broke out with it.

"If you have any poetry to recite at us," Mrs. Sugg sighed, "you might as well get it over—"

"Only the sign above the door of the university library," Geraldine said, twinkling:

> *Sit here and read, and read again*
> *Until you have been rested;*
> *But kindly don't forget to note*
> *That SILENCE IS REQUESTED.*"

Then Geraldine Harrison gave us a somewhat saucy wink.

Hoping to bring her down a peg or two, Old Man Unrath said, "Girly, just how familiar are you with that Dewey Decimal System, or whatever it is?"

"Reasonably familiar," Geraldine replied. "Basically, all recorded knowledge is divided by ten, and then—"

"Thank you, Miss Harrison." The judge swept in. "And what innovations do you foresee for the up-to-date twentieth-century library?"

"Well, of course the photostat that has recently come on the market." Geraldine turned over a kid-gloved hand.

"The photostatic copy is the innovation of the age."

Old Man Unrath erupted at the thought of such expense. "Photocopy my—"

"Now, now," the judge restrained. "A photostat or any such machinery is well beyond our means, Miss Harrison. Who would pay for such things?"

"I would." A man with an imposing backside rose from the front row. "Basil D. Harrison," he said, turning to command the room. "I am Miss Geraldine Harrison's father, and I will gladly provide an up-to-date photostat machine to help my daughter better serve this community."

The room fell mute. If this father was good for a photostat machine, what could we get out of the other fathers? They might start bidding up their daughters. Endless shelves of new volumes stretched across our minds, and separate desks for Circulation and Registration and I don't know what all.

Another big man was on his feet. "Herman R. Fulwider," he called out. "Indianapolis. All the shelving you can use, when my daughter Lodelia is your librarian."

The crowd roared. The back-row signs drooped.

A third father was up. "Gerhard Stutz, Grace's dad. A complete lighting system to your specifications, and, of course, to Grace's."

We were electrified. The six eyes of the board turned to the final father.

He rose. "Cecil M. Ridpath, and I present to you . . . my daughter, Irene."

Irene mounted the platform. Beside me, Jake had forgotten to breathe. I think she saw us. She sent a small smile our way. Her little three-cornered hat dipped down over a lens of her pince-nez. On her well-tailored bosom hung the same gold pin all the other girls wore, no doubt their sorority badge.

"Irene Ridpath." She had hobbled handily. Now she sat smoothly.

"Let's speak plain," Old Man Unrath plunged in. "I'm no book burner, but half the books in this library ain't fit to read." Amens rose from the rear.

"Then read the other half," Irene replied.

Old Man Unrath faltered. Mrs. Sugg moved in. "Miss Ridpath, as to your quali—"

"We all have the same qualifications." Irene nodded to the front row. "We have mastered the classification system and its application to the card catalog file. We have actually read the books. You would be lucky to have any of us."

And we'd thought Geraldine Harrison was confident.

"What, in your opinion, Miss Ridpath, makes a great librarian?" the judge wondered.

Irene pinched off her spectacles. "I can only quote the words of Melvil Dewey, of the Dewey Decimal Classification." She stood then and began to quote: "'To my thinking, a great librarian must have a clear head, a strong hand, and, above all, a great heart. And when I look into the future, I am inclined to think that most of the men who will achieve this greatness will be women.'"

This brought every woman in the place to her feet, including Aunt Hat.

"I will have order in this court!" rapped Judge Ransom, forgetting where he was. When we all settled down, he said, "And, Miss Ridpath, what makes you think that you are, ah, the man for the job?"

Irene looked up in a show of surprise. "But you need not choose among us," she told the trustees. "You can have us all. We'll take turns and double up at busy times. It will be good experience for us and even better service for you. We'll share the job and the salary, four ways."

Something like sunrise dawned across Old Man Unrath. It was the bargain of the century, and his old pink eyes were wet with greed.

The cat had Mrs. Sugg's tongue, but the judge wanted to be certain. "Are you sure the other young ladies—"

"Oh, yes, it is all for one and one for all, in our sorority and in the sacred pledge we have made to the Library Science department. We even have our own Librarian's Hymn, you know."

We didn't, but now Irene summoned up the other three. They grouped themselves like a barbershop quartette, and burst into song, in very close harmony:

"Gently, reader, gently moving,
Wipe your feet beside the door;
Hush your voice to whisper soothing,
Take your hat off, I implore!
Mark your number, plainly, rightly,
From the catalog you see;
With the card projecting slightly,
Then your book bring unto me,
unto me."

In the hush that followed, Irene pointed to her father, saying, "Now, Daddy."

Ridpath rose again. "Subscriptions to all major magazines in the name of the library, and a subscription to St. *Nicholas* magazine for the kiddies."

Applause echoed.

"New business?" the judge roared, pounding us into submission. "Or further comments from the assembled citizenry?"

"Right here!" Colonel Hazelrigg got up. He was six foot three, stooped. Large birds could have nested in that white thatch.

"I stand with the Honorable Sam Houston, Governor of Texas, who said, 'I am for the Union without any "if"!'"

Aunt Hat jerked on the Colonel's coattails, and the judge declared the meeting adjourned.

CHAPTER SIX
The First Morning of Creation

When it came to spreading our news, a headline in the Indianapolis *Star* said it all:

BEVY OF BIG-CITY BOOK BEAUTIES HITS
PODUNK WITH FORCE OF RECENT TORNADO

The harness shop folded that week. But uptown was otherwise in uproar. We heard how the old library, gutted, was being refitted with fumed-oak shelves and incandescent lights. Just by looking in the new window people said you'd think it was the Kokomo Carnegie. Others said the whole thing was the devil's workshop, from books to lightbulbs. Everybody said: Yes, but who'll pay the upkeep?

Jake and I kept clear of uptown. I'd have to put on a skirt, and he was teaching himself the tungsten filament electric headlamp from a book in his off hours. Besides, his heart was hollow as a rotten log.

The Ridpath Pierce-Arrow had brought Jake lowest. Not all the paving in Indiana could bring Irene's world closer to ours. Which was a doggone shame because he couldn't get her out of his mind.

About the best we could do was keep our heads down and our hopes small. One July morning I was in the grease pit, making the dirt fly, seeing how much I could get done before the heat of the day.

I heard an auto, and the Stoddard-Dayton rolled up. Irene Ridpath looked down at me in my grease pit. When she pulled hard on the brake and turned back her veils, I wanted the earth to claim me. She was peaches and cream and rose petals. I was a severed head sticking up from bald ground.

"Good morning, Eleanor," Irene Ridpath said, like we met every day around this time.

I felt the dirt caking my face and my person. I wanted to burrow into the ground with the other earthworms. But we were in business. "How are you fixed for gasoline?" I sighed, wondering if she knew her way around a dipstick.

"We will need a full tank," she said, "and you'd better have a look at my . . ."

"Grease cups?"

"Probably. And if you can get away, I could use your help." She stood in the auto, and she was wearing a motoring suit with a Norfolk jacket and a skirt slit front and back. She showed a lot of ankle stepping down. Where was Jake? The garage was tomb-silent, but listening hard.

There's no ladylike way to climb out of a grease pit. I threw a leg and heaved, ending up at Irene's shoes, where I sprang to my bare feet. My toenails were crusty, and there was loam between my toes. Irene glanced down and away. The dust she'd raised was still settling in the road from town.

I knew where Jake was—right there on the other side of the garage wall. I sidled over and slammed it with my fist.

He stumbled outside, cradling a fly-wheel, tongue-tied. The sun hit his wavy mop, and his shirtsleeves were rolled up his big arms. He looked like he couldn't believe his luck.

"Jake," Irene said, very matter-of-fact, "I wonder if you could spare El—Peewee this morning. It's time to shelve the books, and since the tornado they've been stored in a certain Muehlbach barn."

A farmer name of Muehlbach with a good tight barn offered to store all two hundred and twenty-five books. Irene said she didn't know where the Muehlbachs lived and they weren't on the telephone.

Somehow Jake let it be known I could be spared. But you could neither scare nor coax any conversation out of him if you were pretty. You had to wait.

"I'll wait," Irene said to me. She meant I better scrape some of the topsoil off me. And there needed to be a skirt on my horizon. And shoes.

My heart thudded in my overall bib. What a sudden place this world is. Here I was, about to go motoring with Irene Ridpath. The day that had started so low, in fact under ground, was heading uphill fast.

At the pump I washed every part of me I could get to. Up in my room I plunged into my school dress. I hurried through my hair and reached for a ribbon to tie it back. I didn't risk a look in the mirror. I didn't want to spoil the moment.

I only hoped Jake wasn't lurking behind his lathe while Irene cooled her heels in the road. I cursed those horse stalls so handy for hiding. The Colonel wouldn't let us rip them out because he said horses would make a comeback. There was still hay in the moldy mow.

But I found them in the back stall. Jake was showing Irene his axles and explaining to her about a steering knuckle. Any young woman who shows interest in a steering knuckle is lying. But Irene managed to pay attention.

Then when it was time to go, she could have bounded up on her running board all by herself. But she put out a gloved hand for Jake to help her up, though he was grease to his elbows.

I saw that it took a lady to show a boy how to be a gentleman. I wondered if I'd have the patience.

"I'm pretty dirty," Jake said.

"It's the kind that washes off," Irene replied, already settled on the passenger's side. "You drive, Eleanor."

"But I don't know how," I said, while Jake hid a small smile.

"Get up in the auto," Irene said.

I was a mile high up here, hemmed in by the big steering wheel. Worse, I'd grown out of the skirts on this dress. My hightop shoes came up only so far. I showed some hide between.

The Stoddard-Dayton was fitted with an electric self-starter. It worked off a storage battery to rotate the crankshaft. I just didn't know how to get the thing going.

"Retard the spark lever." Irene pointed it out.

We'd heard of people being electrocuted—fried alive—by their own self-starters. They were found with their hair tightly curled and the charred remains of a hand on the spark lever.

She showed me the gas lever on the steering post. "Advance the gasoline. Press down gently on the clutch. That's the clutch."

The engine and my heart turned over. The hood pulsed between the big, brass-trimmed acetylene headlamps.

"Release the emergency brake." It stuck up on my left. I squeezed it loose, and the auto rolled forward. I reared back in fear, grappling for the gearbox.

Packard had introduced the H-slot gearbox several seasons back: three forward, one reverse. Irene pointed out a gear, and the Stoddard-Dayton jumped like a flea on a dog. Jake made a big show of dashing back in the garage to save himself. Which wasn't funny. We shuddered ahead. "Is it this direction?" Irene asked.

No, the Muehlbach place was back in the other direction. I wondered if I could get us there by going around the world and coming up on it that way, because I didn't know where the reverse gear was.

"There it is." Irene pointed. "Clutch." I put in the clutch and jerked into reverse. I hadn't thought about steering, but I grabbed the wheel. We lunged backward into the dry ditch. I ground into a forward gear, and we made a half circle in the road and were in the other ditch. But going the right way.

Jake stuck a worried eye out of the garage door. Which wasn't funny.

I fought the wheel, but yanked us onto the crown of the road, heading for town. A lady never sweats. I was wringing wet. Sparks flew snarling out of the weeds, trying to keep up with us to bite our tires and scare us off.

"Is that the dog you never saw before in your life?" Irene called over the engine's roar.

"That's him," I said, "back again." We hummed ahead, on and off the crown of the road. The telephone poles filed past. Their wires sang like a tuning fork.

Luckily, we met no auto or horse. Those on foot dove for ditch and embankment. By uptown, I thought I had her pretty well under control.

I learned to turn, and we rattled over the interurban tracks, aimed south. It was only a mile of straight, graded road to the Muehlbach place. I pushed her right up to about fifteen miles an hour. The fences fluttered past. There wasn't a cloud in the summer sky, and the corn was knee-high by the Fourth of July. It was like the first morning of Creation.

And I'll say this for Irene: She neither shrieked nor flinched, even when I clipped the Muehlbach mailbox, turning up their lane.

Muehlbach himself heard us coming. Old Man Unrath could have heard us. We sounded like thrashers.

"Brake," Irene advised, "brake," so I didn't hit the barn. But I killed the engine by not knowing when to put in the clutch. Our dust overtook us.

Farmer Muehlbach was a true hayseed, and he didn't have to tell you he kept pigs. There was a tribe of Muehlbachs, and the little ones hung on the fence, too scared to come closer. They may have seen me clip their mailbox.

Irene climbed down and went to work, flattering Muehlbach for the favor he'd done the library.

"Well, we read very little," he allowed. "But we don't mind if others does. We're Methodist."

Then he fell all over his clodhopper boots to show us the books in the barn. A couple sweet smiles from Irene, and he was offering to deliver the books to the library in his own wagon, saving us the trips. As Irene always said, there's nothing any more useful to a librarian than a man with a wagon and a team.

While he went for them, she pointed to the other end of the barn. "Eleanor, is that what they call a chassis?"

It was, more or less. It was the abandoned body of an old Brush runabout, wheel-less. The Brush was an automobile that Ford had run out of business. It had been chain-driven and sold new for under five hundred dollars. The body, the chassis, was made of wood to keep it light and cheap. Hickory and oak, mostly.

"That's the body of a Brush," I told her. "It had a wooden body, wooden axles, wooden wheels and wooden run, as the saying went." Chickens were roosting in this one. Muehlbach was driving a tin Lizzie now, so he'd put the Brush runabout out to pasture.

"Doesn't Jake want a chassis?"

He'd been trying to save for one, a used one. I doubt the Brush would be his first choice, but still . . .

"Shall we get it for him?" she said, meaning she would.

"Jake won't take charity," I warned. "He's proud."

She looked thoughtful. "Pride strengthens a woman, but weakens a man."

"Who said that?"

"I did," she said, and here came Muehlbach.

She had me drive back to the library uptown, and I only hit one animal, just a little one, probably a weasel. But animals were going to have to be more careful here in the automobile age.

The library was a revelation to me. We didn't keep much house, Jake and I. I'd never been anywhere this fresh with so many sharp angles and shellacked surfaces. The electric lights hung down like globes in a galaxy. The photostat machine was modern as tomorrow.

Irene had already stood up the twenty-five volumes she was donating of the Ridpath Library of Universal Literature. Naturally, she was from a literary family. And she'd brought a new blotter for Miss Dietz's desk.

Then after Muehlbach brought the books, Irene had us arranging them according to the Dewey Decimal System.

"Miss Dietz didn't have them like that," I remarked. "She arranged the books by size."

"I see," Irene said. "You were a faithful library patron?"

"Not after I got banned from the place for life at the age of ten."

"Why?" Irene asked. We were wearing big aprons, matching.

"I wanted to check out a book and take it home, and Miss Dietz didn't like anybody doing that. She liked to keep the books where she could see them."

"Was that the whole reason?" wise Irene inquired.

"I may have used some language on her," I admitted. "I hadn't reached the age of . . ."

"Discretion?"

"Probably."

We worked like troupers until the sun was in the west. She hadn't seemed to need her pince-nez spectacles to read the book titles. *Ben-Hur, Uncle Tom's Cabin, Little Lord Fauntleroy.* You name it, she read it without her specs. I brought this up.

"Oh, they're only window glass," she said. "But they add some dignity, as I am just nineteen."

Now she was talking about a tea to initiate the library. I'd never been to anything resembling a library tea. We didn't have them around here. "Miss Dietz never—"

"No, she wouldn't," Irene said. "You'll be needed as a local hostess, Eleanor. I have a tea gown I never wear now. I have a feeling it will fit you."

My eyes glazed over while my mind wandered to matching shoes. "Will the others be there?"

"Grace, Lodelia, and Geraldine? Naturally. They'll soon be reporting for duty. Presently, they're floating on Lake Maxinkuckee in canoes with beaus."

"Beaus? What are they?"

"Suitors. Gentlemen callers. Fraternity men with ukuleles."

"Oh." I strove to picture this. "Are they spooning?"

"Or reading aloud," Irene said.

I was catching glimpses of me now in Irene's gown at a library tea. "Say, you wouldn't be trying to make a librarian out of me?" I said, suspicious.

"Nobody can make you into anything," Irene said. "That's your job."

She drove me back home through the gloaming. Halfway to the Hazelrigg Settlement she set her brakes and stared into the ditch. "It looks as if somebody has abandoned a large accordion."

I leaned out and saw. "Them's Mrs. B. D. Klinefelder's corsets."

Irene blinked. "How do you know?"

"Everybody knows. Her wash was on the line when the tornado touched down. It's all over town. A tornado's a funny thing. We found one of her big garters wrapped around the knob on our privy door."

Irene gazed fascinated at me before grinding into a gear. Life here was nothing like Indianapolis.

I liked to never settle that night. I stretched sleepless on the cot as the telephone poles flashed past my brain. That first day at the wheel of an automobile sang in my soul, and the open road stretched before me.

I was awake again at the sound of breaking glass. Outside somewhere, Sparks growled and howled. I hit the floor and heard Jake pound down the porch steps. The sound had come from the garage, that big window on the side.

From my sill I saw Jake running down the yard wearing very little, carrying a tire iron. But distant figures swarmed low through Aunt Hat's melon patch up above, making their escape.

So that particular party was over, at least for tonight. I wondered what they got this time. Did we know who they were? Near enough.

I fell back in the bed and dreamed I was pouring punch into crystal cups at a library tea. I was wearing my old cap and seemed to be in the grease pit. But I had on Irene Ridpath's tea gown, and I looked real good.

CHAPTER SEVEN
The Price of Progress

At the other end of July, a parcel came from Railway Express. Jake hardly looked up from his gear casting as I cut out for the house. In my room I made the unwrapping last: brown paper, then tissue, then a box emblazoned with *L. S. Ayers & Company*.

Inside a white drift of paper was a dress, lavender as Irene's letter paper. Me and lavender? I'd never thought, but it was asking to be lifted up. And it unfolded, store-bought, before me. There was lace around the neck, and a satin sash, and a good deal of cross-stitching. What was it doing in a room like this?

Then I saw the shoes in more tissue paper, white patent leather with pearl buttons, and heels. Heels. And packets of silk stockings, lavender to match, with spares.

How long did it take me to know that these weren't Irene's castoffs, that she'd bought them new for me?

How long did I skulk and simper on my cot, keeping this secret, before I tore downstairs and off the porch, vaulting out of my overalls? Screened by the house, I scrubbed myself raw with lye soap under the pump, standing in a pan of suds to wash my feet.

It was all but evening when I wobbled down the yard. Squirrels flickered in the trees. Lamplight played through the chinks in the boarded-up garage window. What was the use of replacing it? I stole inside, along the stalls.

Jake didn't notice. He was standing in the frame of his automobile, between the axles, imagining it was finished. He stood where the driver would sit, if there was a chassis. He gripped air and turned a phantom steering wheel. I knew right where he was—rounding the grandstand curve at the Hendricks County fairgrounds track.

He looked up, guilty from his dream, and saw me edged by lamplight. The satin sash hobbled my lavender skirts. The lace lay in points around my throat. I put forth a foot to show a lavender ankle and the heel on the shoe. I'd had a go at my hair.

What did Irene do with her hands? Mine just hung down.

Jake's eyes were a little cloudy with some mist.

"It's not me," I said. "It's not a bit like me. But I wish . . ."

"So do I," Jake said.

We both wished Mama could see me.

Bills on every pole announced the two great events of the dog days that summer, the library tea and the Hendricks County fair.

Tea talk ran riot as day after day Railway Express delivered crates of books. They were donated from the personal libraries of the Stutzes, the Fulwiders, the Harrisons, and the Ridpaths, to fill out our new shelves.

Though I personally thought time was standing still and history had stopped, the afternoon of the tea came round at last.

Geraldine Harrison and Lodelia Fulwider arrived early in the Peerless limousine behind a chauffeur and footman. The tonneau was heaped with cut flowers, and Geraldine held a punchbowl wrapped in a Spanish shawl, with candlesticks.

Grace Stutz drew up at the hitching rail in a spanking new 1914 Stutz Bearcat, fresh from her papa's factory. It had a six-cylinder overhead valve engine. And this particular Bearcat was enameled in ivory with morocco leather seats. Though I'd have thought Grace's mind wandered too much for driving, there she was up behind the wheel, smiling and being as pretty as usual. She stepped down from her running board, showing the best ankle of the entire bunch.

Irene pulled up in the Stoddard-Dayton packed with the refreshments her servants had prepared in the Ridpath kitchen.

Then there I came up the road in a new dress and old boots, my new shoes swinging in a sack to spare them. I was on my lonesome, Jake being unwilling to turn up at anything as terrifying as a tea.

A crowd was gathering on the planks outside. When Irene saw me, she beckoned me under the ribbon across the library door. Mrs. Sugg had demanded a ribbon so she could cut it.

"Here is Eleanor," Irene said to the others, who hadn't noticed me as anybody else. Grace arranged the flowers. Lodelia, too serious for tea, was already repairing a book with glue pot and sponge. Geraldine and Irene and I set out the eats and mixed the punch. They'd thrown the Spanish shawl over the card catalog that the cold corpse of Miss Dietz had been found under. She was under there a day and a half, as people rarely went into the library in those days. But no need going back over all that.

I'd advised a box of sawdust for spitting. Afterwards, they were glad.

Aunt Hat had sent a long pan of her gingersnaps, homely and brown amid the pale icing on the Indianapolis cakes. She'd no more brave a tea than Jake would, but she may have confused it with a church supper, where everybody kicks in. She'd also kept the Colonel at home, which did us a public service.

At the final moment, the new librarians all vanished into the storeroom. By and by they stepped out again, toes pointing, all wearing tea gowns in summer shades. Their tassels swept the floor. Some of their necklines were low. Grace wore an artistic string of amber beads. They all took my breath away. Remember, Miss Dietz was my idea of a librarian.

The shimmering room robbed me of breath too. And the cakes arranged in patterns and the radish roses and the cut-glass bowl brimming with punch and lump ice. It wasn't anything like here. It was how I'd pictured Indianapolis—with nothing plain and a party every afternoon and music playing in your mind.

Someone touched a match to the candles in silver sticks. Their yellow light played over the gilt bindings on the new books. Outside, Mrs. Sugg took scissors to the ribbon, and we were in business.

"You pour, Eleanor," Irene said, and fear gripped me.

The first through the door were the library trustees and the judge's wife, Mrs. Fern Ransom. She and Mrs. Sugg pretty much ruled the roost in this town. But Mrs. Ransom's face fell when she beheld the scene. Her gaze dropped on necklines and the tea sandwiches rolled up into pinwheels. She may even have noticed the books. She saw her rule here had come to a quick end.

"Well, ain—isn't this nice?" she said faintly. "Just like home."

"Not much like your home, Fern," Mrs. Sugg remarked.

A mob pushed in behind them, all eyes. Candles put people in mind of church, so farmer caps came off. The atmosphere changed sharply when several Muehlbachs showed up. I'd gone to Hoosier Grove with three or four of them and a couple Rileys, all the Rennebargers, and Crystal Fenster. Elwood Soper and Crandall Boggs were conspicuous for their absence, as usual.

"That you, Peewee?" Wilma Boggs said, in her knife pleats. She knew it was me all right, but several didn't. They knew my hair, but couldn't place the rest. Some no doubt wondered who in the dickens I thought I was. The dress seemed to spell the last of Peewee. Yet, it was still me, under it. More or less.

I ladled and poured out of the cut-glass bowl, and put the cups into many a grubby hand. "Smile," Irene said, passing by. "You're too pretty not to." So like a fool I let my eyes fill up, but kept ladling.

Word had traveled from porch to porch as it does that there was grub enough for the county. Even those uncomfortable this near books ganged in. There was even some spotty conversation, everybody asking everybody else if it was hot enough weather for them.

A crowd including Old Man Unrath surrounded Lodelia Fulwider's demonstration on how to fold a protective cover for a library book. People watched her skillful hands and excellent manicure.

Others stared up openmouthed at the electric lights. You got very little electricity around here, let alone frosted glass globes. Nobody took a book off a shelf, but several women stooped for a better look at the handkerchief points on the librarians' skirttails.

All the while, the new librarians nodded like flowers and moved through the room like a waltz I tried to keep time to. Even though it wasn't a bit like me.

The afternoon seemed to tick over pretty good when out of the storeroom rocketed Manfred Muehlbach. Hard on his bare heels was Ethel Ann Riley. They were six or seven, the age to get underfoot. Ethel Ann was at the top of her lungs. "Now you done it, Manfred Muehlbach!" she roared. "You done flooded out the place, and they'll have the law in!" She stamped a broken boot and shook a fist at him. "You'll do time!" she piped.

They swerved my way, and I grabbed for the punch-bowl. Manfred stopped dead, looked for his mother, who wasn't there, and burst into tears. His face seemed to erupt and run down his overalls bib.

Geraldine Harrison and Grace Stutz were soon beside him, and he turned his face into their tea gowns, sobbing. I thought I could nail the problem. Off the storeroom was a strictly modern new restroom with a water closet. With no business to be in there, Manfred and Ethel Ann crept in, and he pulled the chain that flushed the toilet, scaring them both witless. They thought he'd broke the dam.

Irene was near me. "He never saw a flush toilet," I told her. I hadn't seen a lot of them myself, and never sat down. Irene gave me one of her long, thoughtful looks. What she didn't know about our ways would fill those shelves.

She tried to lead Manfred back to the storeroom to show him how a toilet flushes. But he couldn't chance it. He still thought she'd arrest him, and Ethel Ann hoped to heaven she would. He set his heels, and as quick as he worked loose from Irene, he was out the front door, over the hitching rail, and traveling. You couldn't see him for dust.

But that's the price of progress, I reflected, looking down at my punch. Something stirred itself at the bottom of the bowl. I looked closer and noticed it had legs. As it was about the same color as the punch, I might have missed it in a fuller bowl. Maybe I had. I saw now it was a small toad.

Somebody had slipped it in, possibly when Ethel Ann was yelling the place down. Several Rennebargers were on hand, so it could be one of them. A boy, of course. A toad in a bowl of punch has boy written all over it. But he'd been gone too long to nab.

I ladled for the toad and in two swipes had him. Then he was out of the punch, fixing to leap from the ladle, when I dashed him to the floor and flattened him under my shoe. And was ready with my smile when Mrs. P. K. Prevo stepped up for a glass of punch. I gave her one.

Things settled down then, except for a small fire that licked up in a wastepaper basket, so Walker Sugg was somewhere about. But I quenched the flame with a ladle of punch.

The crowd hung on till the refreshments gave out. Judge Ransom circled the room like a bald-headed buzzard, campaigning till the last dog died. Mrs. Sugg and Mrs. Ransom butted heads one last time and withdrew. Finally we had the place to ourselves. As most people took their paper napkins for souvenirs, there wasn't much to sweep up apart from a toad of two dimensions.

The librarians changed back into their driving clothes. Lodelia's chauffeur and footman came from the pool hall to load her limousine. Irene locked up behind us, saying to the others, "It will be uphill work bringing enlightenment to this community, but, girls, we have learned more today than in three classes of Library Science at the U."

And they naturally agreed as they always did with her.

Geraldine and Lodelia rolled away in the big Peerless, waving and drawing the silken blinds against the setting sun.

Irene said she'd drop me back home on her way, though it wasn't on her way. Then Grace couldn't get her Bearcat going. Already a crowd of loafers was gathering. I swung down out of the Stoddard-Dayton before Irene could think.

It wouldn't be Grace's battery, not in a brand-new auto. Besides, she'd get it started, but couldn't keep it turning over.

"Let's see under your hood," says I, strolling up.

And who's coming from the other direction but big Leo "Lug" Kirby of Kirbys' MotorKar Kare behind the library. Bull-necked and brainless, bald-faced Lug Kirby with his tool kit already in hand. How handy. Here he was, Jerry-at-the-rathole.

But I was there first.

Under the hood I took off the distributor cap and fiddled with the little rotor inside. I checked this and that, but the engine was showroom fresh. She hadn't put two hundred miles on it.

"It's bound to be in your gas feed," I said, ducking out from under the hood.

Grace was staring over the steering wheel at me like a calf had spoken. Her eyes were saucers. Then I saw she didn't recognize me as Peewee. And of course I'd forgotten I was wearing my lavender tea gown. Though it wasn't entirely lavender now.

Around I went in my heeled slippers to unscrew the gas cap and blow down Grace's tank. I stuck in a finger and tasted it. With the sharp tang of gasoline, I tasted sweet. Even a grit between my teeth that could only be—

I turned on Lug Kirby, who was crowding me from behind, all quarter-ton of him. I felt hot breath on my neck. Hot and bad.

"Back off, Lug," I barked, less ladylike than I looked. To the crowd I called out, "Somebody's poured cane sugar down this tank. Somebody's looking for business."

Nothing will clog a line like sugar, and it's a five-dollar bill to flush it out.

I glared up at Lug, who looked shifty. He could have mashed *me* like a toad, but not with witnesses. Besides, my tea gown confused him. Though not the meanest Kirby, he was the slowest.

"But they're not getting this business," I declared. The crowd shuffled. Nobody crossed a Kirby, but my dander was up.

Irene looked as lost as Grace.

"We'll tow her out to Jake at the garage if you've got rope," I said to her, and she did. Irene's trunk had everything: rope and the latest patented jack and a collapsible canvas pail. Everything strictly up-to-date.

Once we got the autos lined up, I tied Irene's back bumper to Grace's front with one of my better knots. There were plenty of able-bodied men looking on. But did any offer to help? Not with Lug Kirby on the scene.

As we made a stately procession out the Crawfordsville road, I chanced a look back past the Bearcat. Lug was standing in the middle of the road, his knuckles dragging dirt. That big hulk hadn't poured sugar down Grace's tank so Jake and I could have the repair business. Far from it. Lug stood there, squinting, beginning to think. Oh, he was going to be trouble with a capital T, and his brothers too.

CHAPTER EIGHT
Another Think Coming

"You don't mean those Kirby people damage autos to get the repair business?" Irene bristled. The Stoddard-Dayton was straining some, pulling the Bearcat and Grace.

"Not only that," I said, "they got their own loblolly out on the Lebanon road."

Irene sighed. "What on earth is a loblolly?"

"It's a pothole in the road straddle-wide, well watered and hid with gumbo mud. They keep a team of mules in the barn of a tame farmer nearby. Two, three times a day outsiders in autos drive into that loblolly and have to be hauled out, two bucks a time. As a rule, the axle's broke, so they have to be towed into Kirbys' MotorKar Kare."

Irene vibrated. "That's an outrage. Why doesn't Hendricks County fill the hole and drain the loblolly?"

"The sheriff's married to their sister."

As we began to hove into view, Jake was out under the canopy setting up our overnight sign:

IF YOU NEED GAS
COME UP TO THE HOUSE
OR
HONK TWICE

Irene sounded her klaxon and fluttered a wave, no doubt weakening his knees. Then he caught sight of the Stutz Bearcat with Grace Stutz herself in tow behind.

It would have been Jake's first time this near a Stutz Bearcat, let alone one with hand-sewn upholstery and custom paint. It was the Bearcat of all Bearcats, personally knocked together for the heiress to the Stutz automobile empire. Grace herself sat in the driver's seat with no need to steer. Her hands were gathered gracefully in her canvas lap, her face a vision. Jake gaped.

It took us very little time to put him in the picture and point the finger of blame at Lug and all the Kirbys.

The job was to flush out the Bearcat's gas line. Forgetting all else, I was about to get to work alongside Jake when Irene caught my upper arm.

"No, Eleanor," she said. "We are going up to the house to see if we can save your dress."

I looked down my mostly lavender finery. Without a thought, I'd have dropped down and rolled under the Bearcat. Jake was already there, admiring the pan and the drive shaft.

But somehow I didn't want Irene to see the house and how we lived. I wasn't ashamed exactly. But there'd be boot clods on the porch because I never swept.

But in that way of hers, she said, "To the house," and off we went.

It was getting on for evening, one of those long summer evenings when dusk strolls up the hedgerows, dropping in on every little glade. We never lit our front room anyhow, rarely went in there. It had only two platform rockers and a horsehair settee that Mama and Papa had gone to house-keeping with. And the last of the rag rugs Mama had made. Only one picture hung on the wall, the one of the lone wolf baying at the starry night across the snow.

Afternoon still showed at the window of my room up under the eaves. "That's where I watch at night when the Kirbys come to break us up and steal our stuff," I told Irene. "They want us out of business before the hard road comes through." What I didn't say was that it'd be open warfare tonight, after that little trouble this afternoon with Lug.

Irene only listened. Listening was one of her talents.

She had nowhere to sit but my cot. There was nothing in the room but a three-legged chiffonier. My duds hung on nails. I tried to picture what Irene's bedroom was like. Then I tried not to.

"Slip out of your dress, Eleanor," she said. "I'll show you a tip for removing stains with baking soda and . . ."

She fell silent because I just stood there. Dark was falling, but not enough.

"I don't have no—any petticoat on underneath," I said.

Her hand flew to her mouth. She was blaming herself for not sending petticoats with the dress.

"Of course it was a warm day," I said. "The dress on its own was gift enough, and the shoes."

"You earned them." Irene's voice wobbled.

I only smiled. "Them would be two weeks' work, not an afternoon tea party. You know we're proud, Irene. Too poor for underwear, but proud as Old Nick. Church mice offer us charity, but we won't take it. Jake won't even take money off Grace to blow out her fuel line. Jake's shamed that the Kirbys did that to her. It shames this town."

Irene stood at the window, gazing out, meaning for me to get changed behind her back.

"Then our course is clear," she decided. "We'll have Grace give Jake that auto chassis we saw in the Muehlbachs' barn. It'll be fair and square, without money changing hands."

You had to give her credit for thinking every minute. I

wondered if there wasn't a Library Science course in Scheming. I wondered too how sweet she was on Jake. I took it for granted any young woman would be.

Jake had been showing off to Grace how quick he could unblock her fuel line. From the porch we heard her engine come alive and gun smooth. Not even a backfire. As Irene and I strolled down the yard, we could hear a rumbling voice.

Jake talking to a pretty girl in complete sentences? Voluntarily, without a gun to his head?

He was telling her about an old farmer who lived out from us, Norval Hawkins. He claimed he wanted to be buried in his Ford flivver because it had pulled him out of so many holes, he hoped it could pull him out of that one too.

Grace's laugh trilled up and down the scale as Irene and I rounded the garage. What to my wondering eyes but Jake's foot propped on Grace's running board and his elbow resting on her door, all his fears forgotten.

But it was high time that our librarians took off before dark. With flurried good-byes, Irene sprang up into the Stoddard-Dayton, and Grace looked for her gearshift.

Sadly, she found it. The Bearcat took a standing jump in first gear, lunging at Jake, who barely escaped without tread marks. Grace's head had snapped back, but now she stood on her brake. But it wasn't there. The Bearcat was on the prowl and flattened our IF YOU NEED GAS COME UP TO THE HOUSE sign.

With a bellow and a roar it charged the garage. When it took out one of the supports, the canopy crashed down on its hood with the sound like the crack of doom. Only then did the Bearcat stall. Number three shingles off the canopy roof went everywhere.

Grace, already standing, screamed for heaven to help her and toppled sideways over her door into Jake's arms. Wondrously, he was right there. She hung limp in his grasp, her hat askew, her veils settling. It all happened just that quick, but then you had to be there.

Grace wasn't in a dead faint, because her eyes rolled prettily. But Jake took his sweet time standing her on her pins. Irene was paler than the gloaming. The canopy on the garage had dropped not a foot ahead of where Grace was standing on her brake. She could have been brained or beheaded. Jake was white with rage.

We'd towed the Bearcat out here without realizing that Lug Kirby had not only sugared Grace's gas feed, he'd cut through her brake line. The first time she fired up the car and engaged the gear, she was a speeding bullet that wouldn't stop till it hit something. If she hadn't been aiming at the garage, she'd be mowing down the Colonel's grape arbor by now, making tracks for open country.

Grace was this close to hysterics. Irene wasn't far behind, so it was time to get them both into the Stoddard-Dayton and off home. We all helped quaking Grace up into the passenger's seat. Irene pulled herself together behind the wheel. We watched them out of sight, Jake and I.

The whole front of the garage was a shambles. When we tried to lift the canopy, it broke in two.

"What'll we tell the Colonel?" I said. It was his garage, and he hated automobiles bad enough without this.

Jake studied, stroking his stubble. "We might could say it was Quantrill's Raiders done it."

"When were they?"

"1863."

"That'd be about right," I said.

The Bearcat's hood was creased across, and Grace would have to send the auto back to the plant to have the enamel professionally buffed. But Jake was already repairing the brake cable, in his mind.

We had a long night to get through first. A night no doubt chock-full of Kirbys. Jake looked around for his tire iron. If he thought he was sending me up to the house out of harm's way, he had another think coming.

CHAPTER NINE
Under a Kirby Moon

We meant to spend the night in the crippled Bearcat, Jake and I. How else were we going to protect it? After all, it was worth more than the garage itself and everything in it. And our house. And the Hazelriggs' house. It was worth more than the entire Hazelrigg Settlement put together. We brought down ham sandwiches and cold potato cakes and camped out on the front seats with a big chamois for a tablecloth.

The August night was hot as day, and there were chiggers. We were still parked in that area the canopy used to cover, under a blanket of stars.

You could have read the Brownsburg *Bugle* by the light of the rising moon. A real Kirby moon. I noticed the tire iron across Jake's knees.

"You had a choice," he said after a long silence.

"What choice?"

"You could have backed down. You could have let Lug have the repair business."

"Would you have?" I stuck out my chin.

"No, but I'm a—"

"Don't say it," I said. "I didn't have no more choice than you. Besides, Irene was right there behind me, taking it all in. Irene thinks women ought to stand up for themselves."

"Yes, and Irene's tucked up in her bed in Indianapolis," Jake said, "while you're in the great out-of-doors, waiting for Kirbys."

But when I glanced sideways at him, he was grinning.

"Anyways," I said, "you're getting a chassis out of the deal, though it's only a Brush."

"How do you know that?"

"I looked in my crystal ball." I gave a little shrug like I knew pretty nearly everything there is to know.

"Well, look in it again," said Jake, "and see if you see any Kirbys."

But the Kirbys were almost upon us. They were only footfalls away. The first we heard was Sparks's bark, from up by the arbor. One sharp bark, then nothing. Then an awful scream, like nothing on earth. It spiraled toward the moon. I grabbed my ears. Jake tensed.

Then the worst sight that ever I'd seen. And remember,

I'd seen corpses unearthed in the graveyard. Something aglow shot from around the garage, making for the road. Like Moses's burning bush, but moving. Screaming.

It was Sparks, lit by flames. Somebody had tied an oily rag to his tail and set it afire. You could smell the kerosene from here, and burning fur. Sparks was on fire and trying to outrun it.

He flamed down the crown of the road. Water stood in the ditch, but he didn't know enough to throw himself in. His screams were pitiful, and the ruts glared behind him.

Jake swung down from the Bearcat and lit running. Just like he was expected to do.

I stood up in the auto, and the morocco seat sighed expensively behind me. As a rule, you can't outrun a dog, but Jake was trying. Besides, who knew how much fight Sparks had left in him?

Then from around the garage three figures loomed, backlit by the moon. Right on schedule.

Their lumpy shadows fell across me. Kirbys. Lug for sure and the other two Kirby brothers, Growler and Percy, unless one of them was their dad, who'd ridden with the Younger brothers.

I reached for the tire iron that was down the road in Jake's hand.

They drew up short, not expecting me there. They'd found a way to take Jake's mind off the Bearcat so they could finish it off—and our business with it. But lo and behold, here I was, Johnny-on—

"What the—"

I felt puny, and bleached out by the moonlight. And helpless, which I hate.

"Back off, Lug," I said, wobbly into the night, like I could identify him, though he was just one of the misshapen shadows. "I told you before. I'm telling you one more time. Leave this auto be. Also get off our place."

How I got through that brave speech without my voice breaking in two I couldn't tell you. The dreadful three stirred. One spat. In their hands were various bats and irons, to lay waste the Bearcat.

And me. They wouldn't hold back just because I was a girl. They were fair that way. They grumbled together and edged forward. But I was spot-welded to the auto's floorboards. I'd have let them batter me to death and bleed all over the Bearcat upholstery before I'd throw in the sponge. You know me.

Then I saw something silent behind the Kirbys, suddenly there. Big in the dark, and barefoot. A thatch of white hair tossed by night breeze and pure silver in this light. It was Colonel Hazelrigg in a nightshirt big as a mess tent. As I recall, his eyes glowed.

Rising to his gaunt shoulder blade was his short-barrel Winchester pump action. The moon struck blue fire along its barrels. It would be packed to the gills with double-ought deer shot. Double-ought at one end and three slugs at the back end of the row.

I never drew breath, though the Kirbys kept on bumbling forward. By moonbeam, I saw the Colonel thumb back the hammer and sight down the barrels with an eye like an ember, under a tangled brow.

Just as I was wondering if I was in his range too, the stars shivered, and the night blew up. There'd been only the cricket sound of the Winchester's safety clicking off. Then the shotgun belched orange flame twice and recoiled. It was louder than stump dynamite. Night birds fell off their perches. The Kirbys leapt upwards, climbing their own screams.

The shock alone could have killed them. Their big behinds took most of the shot, and somebody got the slugs. Leftover shot sprayed the garage wall and rattled down the roof. Shot popped like hailstones off the fallen canopy and the Bearcat's hood.

But it was hard to hear or even think, over the Kirbys' howling. Their irons and brickbats fell away from them, and they danced together, trying to work out of their skins. It had to be worse for Lug, who had a behind the size of a sagging settee. But they were all surprisingly light on their feet. The heels on their hobnail boots cracked in the air. When they jigged around far enough, they were looking up the barrels of the Colonel's shotgun.

Had it discharged both barrels? The Kirbys darted behind one another for shelter, grunting and lamenting. They glanced off the garage. They tripped over the fallen canopy. Still, their backsides all but glowed with pitted pain.

Outrun that, I thought, recalling Sparks.

He lived, Sparks did. For years. The fur never grew back on his tail or anywhere near it, which didn't improve his appearance. And he was always shy of campfires and Fourth of July sparklers. He was never again any good as a watchdog either, as we were to learn.

How well I remember him cradled with the tire iron in Jake's arms, wet as a drowned rat, as they came back up the road on the run. Sparks had let himself be caught and dumped in the ditch to put him out.

Jake drew up and observed the Kirbys disappearing up the road and the Winchester in the crook of the Colonel's arm. "That had to sting some," Jake said.

The Colonel himself scanned around for more skirmishers. The night breeze stirred his nightshirt higher than you'd care to think about. Jake put the whimpering Sparks down. "Look like Quantrill's Raiders to you, Colonel?"

"Looked like Kirbys to me," the Colonel said, sane as you or me. If he ever noticed the Bearcat glowing like an iceberg in the moonlight, he never said. Or the canopy in pieces. He turned up toward the arbor and home. Aunt Hat could sleep through anything.

Rumor reached us that it took till Thursday for the Kirbys to pick all the shot out of each other's rear elevations. Though you'd hate to picture the scene, the three of them working each other over with steel knitting needles and long-nosed tweezers seemed to keep them occupied and home nights.

By the end of that week, Grace had her Stutz Bearcat back. If its bodywork wasn't factory fresh anymore, the brake line was good as new. As Jake said, he'd either have to fix her brakes or give her a lot louder horn.

He had the Brush wooden chassis out of the Muehlbachs' barn now, and glad to have it because beggars can't be choosers.

Time was running short, and Jake was X-ing out each August day as it came. We were only X's away from the Hendricks County fair and its first-ever ten-mile stock automobile event.

Jake had an automobile to get built, and if it made a showing in the race, or at least finished, it'd be first-rate advertising for us. Already he was dreaming of permanent pumps, a lighted sign, all kinds of improvements that would put our garage on the map when the hard road came through. And so that auto of ours was like a sick child. Jake was up with it all hours.

He had to get the chassis justified to fit the frame, and it was just this much short. Then come to find out, the chassis had woodworm. I went to work with bug killer and sealer, laboring along with him, as helpful as I knew how to be. I like to break my arm six times in six places, cranking that engine alive, time and again.

We sweated blood over the auto and at just the hottest time of year. I'd work every night till Jake ordered me up to the house. Then sunrise would stir me a moment later, and I could hardly lift my head to eat oats, as the saying went. I suppose it was the best time of our lives.

It felt like it. Progress was sending out its concrete feelers to find us where we lived. But just for now, it was Jake and me against the world. So, with grease-blackened paws, I clung to every moment down at the garage. They were the long days of summer, but way too short for me.

Besides, all we knew for sure about the future was that we were due for another visit from the Kirbys, sooner rather than later. But Jake's dream was too big to see around. There he was at the wheel of the car he'd built from the axles up, making the grandstand turn in the middle of the pack and holding his own. Jake McGrath in goggles with his cap on backwards.

And where was I in this dream? Up on the fence, I guessed, eating the dust of the circling machines, breathing fumes. Being Jake McGrath's sister, I guess.

PART TWO

A Bucket of Bolts and a Dream

CHAPTER TEN
Blinded by Pride

We rolled our automobile out of the garage one hopeful August morning. It was time for a true road test, with the world watching. We'd left it till late, for tomorrow was race day at the fair.

Now Jake was calling the dirt between garage and roadside once covered by the canopy our "forecourt." As quick as the sunshine struck the former Brush chassis, the wood grain gleamed like an old stage coach. The hood was tied in place with authentic leather straps whittled from a harness we found in the haymow.

The two seats were wicker, with a story of their own. We'd found them, a pair of legless chairs, out in the dust of the forecourt when we opened up one morning. They looked very like two old wicker chairs off the Hazelrigg porch, cut down for the auto, though the Colonel was dead set against all motorcars on principle. On one of the chair seats was a fresh peach pie still oven-warm, peaches now coming into season.

We were blinded, Jake and I, by sunlight, and pride. "What shall we call this machine?" I pondered, to test him. "It ought to have a name. Should it be 'The Irene' or 'The Grace'?"

But he wouldn't rise to my bait. What I knew about how the opposite sex thinks, you could put in your grease cup. "We could call it 'The Peewee,'" he said, breaking off a piece of pie crust.

"The Peewee?" I said, falling for it. "How come?"

"Because it's noisy but hasn't been around much."

I snapped a chamois at him, but I was all set to go.

"Not looking like that," Jake said. I busied myself polishing coachwork.

"I said, not looking like that," Jake said. "Are you getting deaf as Old Man Unrath?"

"I hear you," I said, "but it goes in one ear and out the other."

"Nothing to stop it," Jake said.

So I had to go up to the house and change into a durn dress. From there I heard Jake down in the yard, his head under the pump, trying to sing "Come Away With Me, Lucille, in My Merry Oldsmobile." He was soaping seriously, so I took it that our road test would include a pit stop at the library.

"I'm cranking," I said, "dress or not." Jake deserved to be behind the wheel, where he was advancing the spark. The auto roared in a thin, raggedy voice. The crank missed my elbow by an inch, and I dropped into the other wicker seat.

Jake shifted into first gear, smooth as butter, almost. We began to roll, jittering till we found the ruts. With neither roof nor windshield, nothing stood between us and blue, dappled morning. The world slipped under us and fell wavering away. Jake pulled into second, and though the clutch was still slipping, we almost surged. He found third, and we flowed like the Wabash River, nearly. There wasn't a cloud in the sky. We were somewhat oversprung, but our hearts were bouncing anyway.

We didn't meet a soul between here and town, which was provoking. Not even Mrs. Olive Sugg, who could never stay home. There seemed to be birdsong, though we couldn't tell without a muffler. The engine had gone from a stutter to a snarl. We swept past Beulahland, loud enough to wake everybody in it. In mere moments the hitching rails of uptown were in full view.

Irene and Grace, on duty that day, were standing outside the library. Evidently they'd heard us from afar. Jake killed the engine, and it died a loud death, with an almighty backfire. Smoke rose. We were already drawing a crowd.

All business today with their hems pinned up, Grace and Irene wore paper cuffs. They were running a summer reading club for little kids, Muehlbachs, mostly. They invited us in.

Jake wasn't easy about leaving the auto unguarded. A bunch as big as a farm auction was standing around it now. Irene had given The Peewee only a glance. Grace, being from an automotive family, lingered longer. Stroking her perfect chin, she gazed at our handiwork, never having seen anything quite like it. The hint of a furrow clouded her brow.

Down by the card catalog a gaggle of small urchins sat in a circle with their noses in books. When Irene told you to be still and read, that's what you did.

Coming to the point, she said, "Jake, do you plan to enter your . . . machine in the race Saturday? There's no record of it on the registration list."

She'd know.

Jake looked lost. We both figured we'd just turn up on race day and wait for somebody to wave a flag or something. Registration?

Irene removed her pince-nez specs to rest her nose. Her posture was always top-notch, but something in her sagged. She gazed at the floor, and I read her mind. Though she wouldn't say it, she thought Jake and I were the greenest greenhorns she'd yet come across. Too dumb to pound sand in a rat hole, as the saying went.

"The registration fee is fifteen dollars." She spoke quietly. The library reeled around us. "Fif—"

"And you'll need—what do they call them, Grace?"

"A pit crew," Grace said.

"A pit crew," I said, dimly picturing one. "Well, I can—"

"No, you can't, Eleanor," Irene said. "Evidently it's a man's world at the Hendricks County fairgrounds. If they encountered a female in the pit, it would disturb their universe."

Grace cleared her throat and launched into unforeseen verse:

> *"Let 'em on the pit crew;*
> *Then, and it's the truth,*
> *We'll find the little hussies*
> *In the doggone voting booth."*

We three gazed at her thunderstruck. This was a whole new side to Grace, and where had she learned language like that anyway?

"Well, it's a song they sing down along Gasoline Alley, the mechanics and those people." Grace turned up a pair of dainty hands. "I didn't make it up."

But I couldn't get over the fifteen-dollar registration fee. It disturbed *my* universe to no end. Jake worked his jaw with a scrubbed hand. We'd done all this work, come all this way, only to—

"How are your spares?" Grace said, again unexpectedly.

Jake flinched. "We've got us a couple," which was pushing our luck, as even we knew.

It was time to go on home and cut our dreams down to size. I felt the heavy weight of all we didn't know about the world. *Fools rush in,* is what I thought. Jake was feeling similar. I slipped my hand into his. I didn't know if he noticed.

Then Grace said, "You'll need a sponsor."

Jake was ready to leave. "We don't have one of them either," he said in the voice of a broken man.

"What is one?" I asked because he wouldn't.

"It is usually a corporation—a tire company or a spark plug firm, or, of course, an automobile manufacturer—to pay the expenses of car and driver. Registration, pit crew, that sort of thing."

"But then you're advertising for them and not yourself," Jake said.

"There is glory enough for all," Grace said, "when you win."

Jake's hand worked the back of his neck. "I don't know about winning," he said. "I'd just like to finish in the pack with a decent—"

"You race to win," Grace said, as sure of herself as Irene. Surer. She was candy-box pretty, but hardboiled when it came to autos. She wasn't a Stutz for nothing. "Winning's why we do it. Nobody remembers the runners-up."

Irene blinked and stepped back. But Jake was still very

hangdog. "I don't know where I'd get anybody to sponsor me," he said.

"I do," Grace said. She smiled sensationally.

Hope dawned.

Jake looked up. "But the race is tomorrow afternoon."

"It can be arranged." Grace snapped her heiress fingers, right in his face. "Like that."

In a golden moment, Jake had a sponsor, the mighty Stutz Motorcar Company. And he had it on the best authority. Something besides hope stirred in Jake's heart. As I watched the three of them there at the library door, him between Irene and Grace, I pondered. Could he be in love with two different girls at the same time?

I wouldn't put it past the male sex, but I didn't know. And where would you look up a thing like that in the library?

Outside, the crowd had swamped the hitching rail and threatened to mob our car. "Hey, Jake," some loudmouth hollered, "what is this thing? It looks like wheels on a privy."

"That's right," somebody cackled, "a two-seater."

That was good for a horse laugh all round. On the subject of our seats, Norval Hawkins proclaimed, "Many's the time I've set on the Hazelriggs' porch, shootin' the breeze with the Colonel in one of them chairs. Takes me back. Don't know if it'd take me anywhere else, though."

More horses laughing. Or parts of horses. Naturally somebody divined that much of our auto had once been a

Brush— "wooden body, wooden axles, wooden wheels and wooden run."

We hadn't expected to be laughed at, not after all the work we'd done. We pushed through the mob, yearning for home.

Feet wide and legs braced with my hair in my eyes, I jerked the crank while Jake advanced the spark. The crowd hardly gave me elbow room. Seeing me flustered and trying to crank in a dress was a great entertainment to every loafer in the district. There were naturally no women among them. Women have better things to do with their time.

Then I couldn't get the thing to turn over. I cranked myself wringing wet. The crowd was clapping in unison. One of my stockings was down around my shoetop.

The ranks parted, pushed aside by none other than big Lug Kirby. Big, bulging, and Johnny-on-the-spot.

"Hey girly," he said, "need a tow?"

That was the lowest moment of all, truly.

CHAPTER ELEVEN
Mountains Moving

We got her started. Never doubt it. I'd have cranked till Christmas. I'd have died in the road before I'd take a tow off Lug and the Kirbys. I'd have—never mind, we got her home, though we blew a tire on the way. I had that to fix while Jake tinkered and tuned, into the wee hours.

Now he not only wanted in the running, he wanted to win. So that's naturally what I wanted too. As the hour grew late, I began to wonder who else would be running the race. The Kirbys popped into my head. Of course they'd be in it, and they wouldn't care what they had to do to win.

I talked Jake out of spending the night down at the garage, tinkering, as we needed our rest. I slept off and on.

In the wee hours I thought I heard an auto in the road. Nobody honked twice for gas, so I turned over. I thought I heard a car start up, but way off somewhere. Through the floor, I could hear Jake sawing logs, dead to the world.

In my dreams, the flags of the Hendricks County fair snapped and flapped all night. I awoke with the first rooster and sprang from my cot. The morning was already hot and bee-busy. I fixed us a real breakfast: scrapple and eggs and a big pot of campfire coffee.

We washed ourselves too, taking turns under the pump. I don't know why. It hadn't rained all month. We'd be thick with dust before we were halfway to the fairgrounds. We waited all we could, then set off down the yard. I'd washed my hair, so it stood out like a hedge. Jake's hair was slicked back, and his shaved chin was smooth and blue. We were a couple of dudes ready for anything.

Except what happened.

When we came around the front of the garage, my heart heaved. The doors hung open. The sorry little padlock was in the dirt, busted. Jake smacked his forehead. We looked into the empty cavern of the garage where our auto used to be. It wasn't there. The Peewee was gone. You could see where it went, up to a point. In a confusion of smeared footprints, its tire tracks led out to the road, turning toward town.

Our auto was gone. Gone in the night.

It dealt Jake an awful blow. He doubled over, breathing hard, the heels of his hands on his knees. He was trying not to cry. He was trying real hard not to cry.

All I could think of was Sparks, wherever he was. He never had been worth a durn as a watchdog ever since the Kirbys set him afire.

The Kirbys.

The morning went on around us. Hot breeze sighed in the cornfield across the road. A row of crows on the power line told each other off. A woodpecker was hard at work, somewhere. The day was the same, but our auto was gone. *Stop, thief,* I said down deep in my heart, hopeless.

Nothing mattered now. The world was blurry, though I could hear an auto up the road by Beulahland. It was a Bearcat, from its engine. Jake looked up.

We saw them coming from afar, Grace behind the wheel, Irene beside her. It was Lodelia Fulwider's day to work the library, not that anybody'd be there on the Saturday of the fair. Grace and Irene were way early for the race. But here they came, no doubt to wish us luck.

Oh, look at them coming, bedazzled by morning light— all unknowing, primed for a day at the fair, their straw hats tied on with veils. And the Bearcat thrumming like a banjo, all snowy enamel and sun-kissed brass.

We had to explain very little to them. The sagging garage doors, the busted padlock, the empty space spoke for us. Irene looked more shaken than Grace. But they both grasped that calling in the law wouldn't do us a thin dime's worth of good. After all, the sheriff was married to the Kirbys' sister.

Their sprigged skirts caressed their white-stockinged lower limbs as they climbed down out of the Bearcat. I'd wondered how they'd look at the county fair amid all them weather-beaten farm women and toothless rubes looking over the latest in manure spreaders. But what business did I have at the fair now?

Irene and Grace stood hat-brim close in the dust of the forecourt, conferring behind their hands. They seemed to flip through the card catalogs in their heads. They were up to something, Grace in the lead. I felt sure the day had changed around us, even lurched. Jake remained low in his mind.

But put two librarians' heads together, and mountains move. It was like the time the tornado hit. Once more we were swept up in a whirlwind of superior force. The long and short of it was this: Jake was going to be in the race after all.

He'd drive Grace's Bearcat in the Ten-Mile Stock Auto Event, sponsored naturally by the Stutz Motorcar Company.

And so a new day rose from the ashes of the old one. Jake rode one running board. I rode the other as the four of us tore through the morning, blazing down the byways, making for the fair. I clung like grim death to the search-light mounted on the driver's door. The wind cut my eyes and sang in my ears and dried my hair. True, Jake wouldn't be piloting an auto he'd built himself from a bucket of bolts and a dream. On the other hand, in this Bearcat he had a fighting chance to win.

Grace took the Wesley Chapel corner on two wheels, and you could see the fairgrounds from here. She drew up in a pasture next to the first tent. A flock of flivvers nested among the horses and farm wagons. We all peeled off the Bearcat and staggered on solid ground.

As we were way early, Grace told Jake to take her car on a good run up and down country roads, to get the feel of it. He was still dazed by his loss, but putty in her hands. From under the driver's seat she drew out a pair of gauntlet gloves for him.

"The wheel and gearshift heat up at racing speeds," she remarked.

Jake wore a hickory shirt and bib overalls, though clean. But Grace drew forth snow-white overalls. She had an extra pair of goggles he was to wear around his neck to keep handy when his own goggles fogged up with dust or splintered from gravel. She showed him how to lower the windshield flat to the hood so he wouldn't go through it in case of accident. You never saw a better organized girl. Irene just stood there.

After Jake had stepped into his official overalls and roared away, we three had a look at the fair, though my mind wasn't on it. But Irene and Grace had free bookmarks to hand out, telling people about our public library.

There was a merry-go-round for the kids, powered by a mule on a treadmill. Farm implements littered the landscape, and the Massey-Ferguson people distributed complimentary cardboard fans. The Pigeon Creek log cabin of the Lincoln family was re-created entirely out of corncobs. On a block of ice in the Dairy & Poultry tent was a bust of President Wilson carved from butter. It was that kind of setup, hayseed heaven.

In the thin throng we saw Aunt Hat, wearing the dog-gonedest sun bonnet. Her skirts and trousers were cinched up by her web belt. A canteen hung off it. She was wandering out of the Jellies & Preserves tent with a glass of grape jelly in each hand. Her own grapes hadn't made this year because the tornado had reduced her arbor to tendrils. Hard on her heels was Mrs. Fern Ransom, the jellies judge. She snatched both jars out of Aunt Hat's hands and stalked back under the tent flap.

Aunt Hat's motto was, "Get aplenty while you're gettin'," and she never troubled herself much over what was yours and what was hers. Besides, if her grapes had made, she'd give you some. And as we know, she robbed the dead.

An excited buzz from the racetrack turned the tide of

fair-goers. We followed, cleaned out of our bookmarks. The mile track was far bigger than the fair. It had been gouged out of the ground years back for sulky racing and never improved. The grandstand, like a giant hen coop with rickets, was filling fast. Grace led us up to a bleacher above the judges, where you could see everything.

The pit crews were set up at trackside. Some of them looked like two or three cousins of the driver, four or five spares, and a can of extra lug nuts.

But directly across from us at the half-mile marker waved the pennants of the Stutz pit crew under a big tent striped in Stutz colors. Seven mechanics in matching overalls worked among the polished tools on a portable table between a high pile of new spares and drums of gas and oil. And would you believe it? The mechanics wore white gloves. Looked like they could take out your appendix between laps. Beside me, Grace preened slightly. The whole Stutz operation was like the Indianapolis Motor Speedway. I wondered how this bunch would have felt about working on our homemade model. But we'd never need to know now.

Irene scanned the crowd milling down by the track.

"The Indianapolis *Star* newspaper has sent both a reporter and a man with a camera," she observed. "How unusual. I wonder who could have alerted them."

Grace straightened her pleats, saying nothing.

Then who turned up but the Kirbys, a pit crew in themselves. A pair of them, Lug and Percy, unfurled a giant banner reading:

KIRBY MOTORCAR KARE KREW
SPONSORED BY

The Acme-Akron Tire Company

&

Fire-Forever Spark Plus,

which made sense, as they were big customers of both firms. They'd be bigger customers still, once the hard road came in. But being Kirbys, they bumbled among themselves, and their big overalls didn't begin to match.

"Kirbys," I muttered darkly to Irene and Grace. "Crooks with a capital *K*."

Being the first of its kind, the race seemed to have few rules and only one flag. There was a fifty-dollar purse, but you had to finish all ten laps, so they weren't figuring on paying out. Not with a track in this condition. It was rutted like a plowed field and a foot deep in dust.

A couple, three autos drew up: an elderly Stevens-Duryea and a dog-eared Apperson Jackrabbit. But a Brownsburg driver was behind the wheel of a spanking new 1914 Chevrolet, with twenty-four horses under its hood.

Then who rolled up but Growler Kirby at the wheel of an aluminum-bodied Marmon, nearly new. The crowd craned. A Marmon Wasp had won the first International Sweepstakes 500 race.

"That's one fast machine," I admitted, though Grace would know that. The Chevrolet could make you eat dust and swallow soot too.

That's when Jake McGrath drove onto the field in the gold and white Stutz Bearcat, catching the sun. The grandstand gaped. I couldn't see the expression on Lug Kirby's moon face, but his knuckles dragged the ground thoughtfully. Growler had to drive the Marmon. Lug himself was too fat to fit and Percy was way too fat.

But who was looking anywhere but at Jake McGrath, with his cap on backwards and the extra goggles slung around his neck and his white overalls blending with the Bearcat? My brother, Jake McGrath, the best-looking boy in Hendricks County, and probably Boone.

I yearned to be closer, down there on one of the straw bales that banked the curve. Shoot, I wanted to be in overalls down among the Stutz crew. You know me. But Irene's hand closed over my wrist.

The Bearcat was in the pit, where the crew swarmed over it. While Jake gunned in neutral, they tinkered with the carburetor, tightening the screw to control the gas flow that leaned the mixture. Even from here, you could hear the engine singing like a lark. They checked over the tires. Bearcat wheels were tricky, with only a single lock nut on them.

Now all the autos were pulling away from their crews, lining up, and Jake and Growler were cheek by jowl at the starting line. The grandstand fell quiet. You could hear people talking over on the midway.

A big shot stepped down from the judges' box to announce the race and mention the fifty-dollar prize for first finisher, if any.

Then turning his megaphone, he boomed, "Gentlemen, start your engines."

They rumbled alive, some coughing. The Stevens-Duryea had to be cranked.

And the flag flourished and went down.

The Apperson Jackrabbit made a bow-legged leap and stopped dead. The others gunned past us, against a rolling wall of dust. The Chevrolet, the Bearcat, and the Marmon skidded together around the first turn. Oil smoked blue from their tailpipes. There was a considerable stink.

The Stevens-Duryea couldn't do better than thirty-five, even tinkered with, and fell behind. A two-man pit crew was on the track, breathing life into the Jackrabbit before it was lapped. The dust was terrible, but you could make out the white Bearcat and the silvery Marmon.

A man held up a sign reading "2," and they blasted past the grandstand into their second mile. The Chevrolet lost speed and pulled into the pit for a change of spark plugs. The Apperson Jackrabbit and the Stevens-Duryea were now in a well-matched, slow-motion race all their own while here came the Marmon and the Bearcat again.

The whole grandstand witnessed what happened next. It was as Growler and Jake came past us, neck and neck into the third mile, Growler threw a wrench, and it caught Jake on the side of the head. The wrench bounced off his temple and spun away, turning in the air. Jake's head jerked sideways, and the blood in his goggles blinded him. He didn't make the turn.

The Kirby Marmon swept around the curve, and the Bearcat shot straight ahead. Jake hit the brakes because the back end came up. We were on our feet now. Everybody was. The Bearcat bumped off the boiling track, hit slick weeds, and nosed into the pile of straw bales, scattering them. The auto stalled. Jake took flight out of the seat, over the wheel. He turned in the air like the wrench, my brother Jake.

CHAPTER TWELVE
Speedette

Grace ran like a deer, down the bleachers, tearing her skirts. Irene and I were hard on her heels. We knocked people sideways and sky-gogglin' as we rounded the track. The auto race went on. The Apperson Jackrabbit chugged past us, though we were almost as fast. In my unhobbled skirts, I could clear the straw bales with daylight between. The Stutz pit crew came on the run from the other direction.

There were people around Jake. He was sitting up, but blood soaked his snow-white front.

I ran a race with Grace to get at him, my mouth drier than a covered bridge. But even from afar I saw his arm, how it stuck out all wrong. The arm he'd lit on.

He sat where he'd landed, amid the strewn straw. The blood branched down from a dent in the side of his head.

But he knew us. Grace's hat was over her ear. Her eyes started with tears. She fell to her knees and reached to lift off the goggles. Now here came a stretcher to carry him to the first-aid tent. And where was I supposed to be?

"Who'd want to be on the pit crew when you could be in the race?" Irene said.

I looked, and she was settling her hat, calmer than Grace or me, far calmer. She glanced back at the Bearcat. Its nose was in the bales like it was feeding. There wasn't any damage that I could see.

But how could I be in the race when it was going on right past me? The gunning engines shook the earth. And I didn't want to leave Jake.

He looked up. "I broke my arm, Peewee," he said, uneven. "It just wasn't meant to be. None of it."

That did it.

"Hand me the goggles, Grace," I said, "and them gauntlet gloves."

A couple of the Stutz pit crew backing the Bearcat out of the bales saw me coming. Who could miss me? I was running flat out, and my red hair stood out a mile around large, round goggles. Somebody was coming up behind me, but whoever it was better not try to hold me back, because I was raring to go.

It was Grace, straw all over her. "Keep your left foot down, use it as a brace," she said, grabbing my arm hard.

"Don't rush third gear. And if you go into a skid, turn into it."

She let me go and gave me a push. Starting back to Jake, she said, "And watch your oil pressure on the gauge."

Then the crew was getting out of my road as I hit the running board and sailed into the driver's seat.

I'd driven an automobile once in my life. And murdered a weasel.

I strained to see through the goggles smeary with my brother's blood. My hand found the self-starter, and the Bearcat growled, still hot from the track. I remembered the clutch and ground into first, making a half-moon in the shattered bales, thumping back onto the track, hoping I was turned the right way. The Stevens-Duryea went past me. Yes, I was going the right way.

I whined into second and geared down to third, taking my time, feeling my way. I could hear the crowd welcoming the Bearcat back. Through the goggles, the world was red-tinted. The Chevrolet was just pulling into the race again.

The ridges on the ruts were trying to twist the wheel out of my hands. The fumes from the other cars were making me silly and light-headed. But I braced with my left foot and gave it the gas with my right. I was flying on the straightaway. But the curve was coming up. I ground down to second gear and rode the ruts around it, leaning well over and making it. Then the straightaway again. The grandstand clapped me past, but I could hear my heart.

Like a gun had gone off in my ear, Growler Kirby's Marmon shot past. He had to be going fifty. I glimpsed his ugly kisser, like a frog in goggles. I'll be all right, I said to myself, if he doesn't have another wrench.

The track smoldered with dust, but there were slicks of black oil. The Chevrolet zoomed by, throwing dirt and caking my goggles just as I was trying to see around the curve. But around it I went, gearing down, and passed the Jackrabbit. But it was dead in the water, and the crew was running out to push it off the track.

I was better than half blind now, and my right shoe was pretty nearly on the floor. The Bearcat was almost full out, and I tried to tell it that it was as good as the Marmon and better than the Chevrolet. I don't know if it heard, but I was coming up on the Stevens-Duryea and wondering how to pass him when his right rear tire blew.

He went into a spin, and I'd hit him broadside if right quick I didn't teach myself how to swerve. The Bearcat leapt from rut to rut, and my rear axle wanted to go into business for itself. For a moment I was on the grass of the infield, but back on the track again as the Stevens-Duryea spun out and turned over.

The crowd hollered, and onlookers fled back from the bales. But I had problems of my own. Dead ahead, the Chevrolet was coming up to pass the Marmon. Growler naturally wasn't going to put up with that. It was hard to see through the brown air, but I was right there on their tails. When they were even with each other, Growler swerved at the Chevrolet. Their front wheels clanked together and threw sparks.

The Chevrolet, going its limit, edged away. Growler took out after him to run him off the track entirely. The Chevrolet driver was mad now. He swerved back and caught Growler off guard. There was a clash and a clatter as Growler's front fender crumpled and his hood flew up and off. It very nearly hit me. Now the Chevrolet and the Marmon seemed locked. They didn't see the oil slick, and of course I couldn't. But they slid through it, linked arm in arm, and I straddled it, which was pure luck.

They were coming up on the curve, banging together, making a tremendous racket, when Growler stood up in the winged Marmon. In his raised fist was a tire iron to brain the Chevrolet drive with. So no, Growler didn't have another wrench.

Making the curve locked to another auto at this speed and standing up to throw a tire iron was a lot to get done if you were trying to be accurate. Still, Growler might have managed it. But a front tire burst with a pop. The tire iron went off into space. The two autos swung around, radiator to radiator, and skidded sideways to a stop that blew all their tires and blocked the track. Growler sprawled over his hoodless hot engine.

I made it round them by inches and took to the infield

again. The crowd roared. The Bearcat roared. I think I may have been somewhat out of my mind. I found the track and zigzagged back onto it. What lap was this? A man was holding up a sign, but who could read it?

I was beginning to know the track now, a dip here, a rut full of oil there. Then ahead there were the Marmon and the Chevrolet again, horns still locked in a dusty lake of leaked radiator water. They were going nowhere. But I'd squeezed around them before and did again, though I left my back bumper behind.

Ahead on the curve it began to dawn on me that I was the only auto left moving. I was chasing myself around this track, around and around. Ten times at least. The wind screamed at me and yanked my hair. My left foot was permanently braced. But my heart throbbed in tune with the engine. And we just kept going, sending walls of flung dirt over the hulks of my old rivals. We kept going.

I'd lost all notion of time when it ran out. As me and the Bearcat came up on the grandstand once more, the groove of a rut grabbed the right front wheel. We veered and swayed. The steering wheel wrenched itself from my grasp, and I heard the lock nut pop when that right front wheel spun off the auto and bounced at high speed up into the grandstand.

The car tipped, and the right front fender and axle plowed a hairpin furrow as the Bearcat swung around and crossed the finish line backwards.

A picture of me, of all people, ran in the Indianapolis *Star* that Sunday. I was still sitting in the Bearcat, at an angle. It's after the race, and I'm all brambly hair and caked goggles. An article ran on the second page of the Sporting section, as follows:

BACKWARD REDHEAD ONLY FINISHER IN RUSTIC RACE

In an upset destined to go down in local history, fourteen-year-old Eleanor McGrath from the unincorporated Hazelrigg Settlement was the only finisher in the Hendricks County fair's first-ever ten-mile stock auto dirt-track event.

She drove, or at least aimed, a customized Bearcat running under the colors of the Stutz company of Indianapolis. The plucky and headstrong miss took over the wheel when her brother was flung out, sustaining a broken arm and facial injuries.

With her pluck augmented by luck, Miss McGrath completed the race and in fact ran a mile over, but crossed the finish line ingloriously, back to front. A wheel, loosened from her machine, climbed the grandstand, where it knocked down and slightly injured

R. L. Bierstadt, photographer in the employ of this newspaper.

What this "win" by a member of the fair sex predicts for the legal posture of women competing against men on American auto racetracks is unknown at this writing.

Fair officials declined to award the fifty-dollar prize to the young Speedette as an unregistered and underaged driver taking over in mid-race. It is to be hoped that the county will invest the prize money in track improvements before another year.

A competitor in the race, Mr. G. Kirby, asked his reaction to being bested by a young girl, replied, "If females was meant to drive, where is it in the Scriptures?"

PART THREE

The Road to the World

CHAPTER THIRTEEN
What I Learned at the Library

A jangle of harness and a stamping of hooves nearly woke me after midnight. But not quite. I'd never been that tired, and got no ease from my dreams. All night long I gripped the wheel of the Bearcat, making the turn, going into a spin. Eating dust and scared out of my wits.

Then it was daybreak with a hint of fall in the air. A turned leaf scudded onto my windowsill. High school would be starting for them who were going. There was more change in the air.

I pulled on my overalls beside the library-tea tea gown, hanging where I could always see it first thing.

At breakfast, Jake was scarcely there. His mind was all loose ends. He couldn't hardly dress himself with that arm in a sling. He was half helpless, and aimless without his automobile, not that he could have done much tinkering on it one-handed.

The look on his face said he had unfinished business all over town, and some of it with me.

Strangely enough, he wasn't as pleased with me as I was with myself for stepping in to finish the race. And make no mistake about it; I was very pleased with myself, though I could have been killed. He slumped over his cornmeal mush and scratched at his bandaged temple.

"If I could just have—"

"But you couldn't, and I could," I said. "We finished, and the Kirbys didn't and the county knows it. That's the main thing. They know it in *Indianapolis*. What does it matter which of us was behind the wheel?"

But it did, a lot. The way the male sex thinks still had me stumped. I didn't mention that as long as he was in that sling, I'd be doing the work of two men down at the garage. Another real good reason I wouldn't have time for high school. Still, he sulked, and it looked all downhill from there.

But then we found our automobile. The Peewee was back, like a horse that had found its way home to the barn.

Jake discovered her. He went outside to throw rocks at something with his good hand, and there she was, drawn up in front of the garage doors, not a scratch on her. A miracle.

I heard him from the house. When I got down to the forecourt, he was doing kind of a dance. Funniest thing you ever saw. I couldn't make head nor tail of it. I'd have bet you the farm that the Kirbys had our auto chopped for firewood by now, or shoved face-first into Raccoon Creek.

There were hoofprints in the dust, and wagon tracks crisscrossing. More mystery. I leaned in across the wicker seats. "Smells like pigs."

"Or Kirbys," Jake said.

But why would they bring our auto back untouched? It wasn't a bit like them. "They may have cut the brake cable," Jake said. I rolled right under, and they hadn't. We were both baffled, but the sun came out and shone all over us.

On Monday morning we couldn't wait to drive it to the library with our news. Jake drove one-handed, but kindly let me crank. We rode funny, after the Bearcat, springy and too light and all over the road. Underpowered, of course. How I'd have raced this thing on a dirt track was anybody's guess.

Of course, when we drew up at the library and backfired to a halt, they were all astonishment.

The rest of that particular August of 1914 seemed to melt and run off in every direction. Turning leaves were everywhere you looked, and the sumac was red. Up behind us black-eyed Susans took over from the hollyhocks. They were laying slab as near us as Beulahland cemetery. The gangs of laborers were mostly farmers working out their taxes by running the road graders and pouring concrete.

You could hear the machinery from here, running right up till dark.

Then with September in sight, the bottom went out of everything. I don't know when Jake would have got around to telling me his news. I learned it at the library.

I'd head on up there whenever I could be spared, oftener after Jake had slung his sling. It was the coolest place to be in this weather, and they could use some help with the shelving. I'd glance through the occasional book too. Presently I was into *Penrod*, a new book by a Mr. Tarkington who was Hoosier like us.

There were only three librarians now. Grace had resigned to put extra work into her studies at Butler U. Or so she said.

I liked watching Lodelia repairing books and mixing her own paste. You never saw anybody so intent. I helped Geraldine send out the first overdue notices, a red-letter day, and I wrote in the addresses. If you didn't bring your books back, she was apt to send her Packard out, even over country lanes, and her chauffeur would show up at your door. Oh, they meant business.

But I looked out for Irene especially. Before I'd met her, all I'd ever been was Jake's shadow. She was the one who'd asked me why I wanted to be on the pit crew when I could be in the race. I still didn't know what to do with this knowledge. But I kept going back to Irene to learn more, and one day I did.

It was a slow afternoon, just the two of us in the library with nobody there but Old Man Unrath reading a *Farm Journal* and deafer than a post. Irene was rubber-stamping a pile of books she called "new acquisitions." Then very offhand, though she was never offhand, she said, "It is an excellent school, the best girls' school in Indianapolis. Grace, Lodelia, Geraldine, and I all went there. And a number of grain dealers' daughters from the outlying districts come in to board."

So what? I thought; then suspicion crept up on me, and Irene wasn't meeting my eye. What did her old school have to do with—

"Oh, for pity's sake," she said, giving a book a savage stamp, "hasn't Jake told you that you're both coming to live in Indianapolis?"

My heart stopped. No, Jake hadn't gotten around to telling me. But the cat was out of the bag now, and Irene had to tell me herself.

Jake was going to work for the Stutz Motorcar Company at their big Indianapolis plant. Electric headlamps were the coming thing, as I knew myself, and Jake had some ideas about the tungsten filament. He had theories about four-wheel brakes too that had come to him while we were building The Peewee. Mr. Gerhard Stutz, Grace's dad, had personally offered him a job. I personally thought Mr. Stutz had little choice.

The afternoon light slanted across Irene's stamping hand.

I didn't know where to start. I felt like a yanked-up weed.

"I ain't a-going," I told her, talking countrified to remind her how backwoodsy I was. "I'm staying put to run the garage. They've laid slab as far as . . ."

But I petered out, and wise Irene let me.

I couldn't run the garage on my own, and what would it be without Jake but a dry husk left over from summer.

So I fetched up a sigh with just a small sob in it, and told Irene, "I'm going to the high school right here." I tried to make it sound like a plan I'd had right along.

It wasn't what she had in mind for me. You could see it in her face. There was some pursing around her mouth.

"You told me yourself one time that nobody can make you into anything. That's your job. It was that day right after I ran over the weasel."

I let her remember.

The wall clock moved toward closing time. A tang of library paste hung in the air. "But where will you live?" Irene asked, quietly.

"Home, as always. The Hazelriggs are right next door."

"Is that the old gentleman who thinks I'm Clara Barton?"

"He has good days," I said. "He has bad." I decided not to bring Aunt Hat into it.

Across the room Old Man Unrath rose from the library table, his knees popping like corn. He shuffled toward the front door. It would kill him outright to have to pay for his own *Farm Journal* subscription. Just outside on the steps stood a dim figure in a bad hat, seeming to wait for him.

"Good grief," I blurted. "Is that Miss Daisy Daggett out there, my old grade-school teacher?" My knuckles tingled.

Irene nodded. "They meet here. They're a match, you know. They have much in common."

True. They were both cranky and cheap. Somehow that reminded me of another couple with a lot in common. Then I knew why I wouldn't be following Jake to Indianapolis. I'd have braved that fancy girls' school. I might even have let them try to make a lady out of me. But I couldn't bear to share my brother. I'd give him up first, and let him go. Though the lump in my throat was growing no smaller.

"This is Grace's doing, isn't it?" I said. "Her plan."

Irene pinched the specs off her nose, as we were alone now. "She's not as silly as she seems. She's very well-organized."

"He was sweet on you first," I said. "Jake was."

Irene colored a pretty shade of peachy pink.

"I thought you might be sweet on him." And why not? He was the best-looking boy in Hendricks County, and probably Boone. And the best. And my brother.

"Ah, no," she said. "That first day down at the garage, I thought of Grace for him. Not only is she a young woman of privilege, motor oil seems to flow in the veins of both of them. They're a match."

"Jake wouldn't marry for money," I warned. "He's proud

as Old Nick. Church mice offer him charity, but—"

"Of course not," Irene said. "But Grace can open doors for his talent. There's nothing she wouldn't do for him. Nothing."

Setting her rubber stamp aside, she reached for the ring of keys on her belt, to lock up.

But I couldn't quite credit it. "Irene, didn't you feel even a little flicker for Jake?"

"Hardly a flicker," she said fairly. "He's certainly the kind of young man I hope to meet one day, though one less mechanical."

"And when will that be?" I supposed she'd know.

"I will want a Ph.D. in Library Science first," she said, locating a key.

"Oh," I said, not knowing. "Do they let women be one of them Ph.D.s?"

Irene drew up. "They don't *let* women be anything, Eleanor. You have to give *yourself* permission."

Don't ask me about the day Jake left and went off to find his future in Indianapolis. I won't tell you. I'd get the page wet, though you know me, I'm no crier.

Anyway, he went, but I kept The Peewee. If I was going to have to go to high school, I sure as shoot wasn't going to walk.

And I lived with the Colonel and Aunt Hat. How long

I'd have lasted alone in our old house I couldn't tell you. As quick as Jake left, Aunt Hat turned up. Being a woman of few words, she just told me to get my stuff and come on over.

It wasn't until along in September that the Kirbys got around to burning down our garage.

They set fire to it one night by the light of a hazy harvest moon, a real Kirby moon. We watched it burn from up on the porch, Aunt Hat, the Colonel, and I. Leaving nothing to chance, I'd been parking The Peewee up behind the arbor, out of harm's way.

Had the Kirbys heard Jake and I'd sold up and shut down? Probably. Everybody knew everything. But they wouldn't want anybody else setting up in business at this location. They were looking ahead. They'd built themselves what they called a "lubritorium" to work warm in all winter on the traffic flowing through on the slab. And they dearly hated competition.

Colonel Hazelrigg sat back in his rocker to watch the fire, pretty satisfied. If he couldn't run it as a livery stable, he'd as soon see the durn thing burn. And the day of the livery stable was over, buried under slab, out to pasture.

When the flames licked up to the mow, the old bone-dry hay went with a whoosh and heat you could feel up here on the porch. It put the Colonel in mind of the time he'd burned Atlanta.

Aunt Hat sat with us, wrapped in her shell pink shroud.

She was picking out black walnuts. The porch floor was paved with them, drying. Her hands were dyed black till next summer.

Where Sparks was, I couldn't tell you. Nowhere near this much fire.

CHAPTER FOURTEEN
The Trunk in the Attic

Aunt Hat and the Colonel weren't as crazy as everybody said, not quite. Either that or I got crazier living with them. They were just being themselves, which was a good lesson for me, or anybody heading for high school.

But nothing about them was like anybody else. Not even their cat. If he had a name, I never heard it. Nobody kept cats except in a barn. But like Aunt Hat herself, the cat wandered around, day and night, in the house and outside, wherever he wanted to go. He was a first-rate mouser, even famous.

One time back when the Colonel still shaved his own shingles and cut his own firewood, the cat got in the way. The Colonel just neatly chopped off one of his forepaws.

He healed, but lost weight and interest. He couldn't catch his dinners, and wouldn't be fed by hand.

So the Colonel whittled a realistic little wooden paw for him and cut a thong to strap it on. That's all the cat needed. Ever after, when a mouse looked out of a hole, the cat could snatch it with his good paw and knock it in the head with his artificial one. You never saw anything like it.

But he was standoffish, especially around anything sharp. Occasionally, though, he'd slink up to my room at night and do me the honor of sleeping at the foot of my bed, in a circle of himself with his head propped on his wooden paw.

It was from this household I went forth every morning to high school, and it wasn't too bad, really. From the first morning, I was that girl who'd finished in the Hendricks County first-ever ten-mile stock automobile event—backwards.

I was the only girl, possibly in Indiana, who roared up to school every morning in a car handmade by her brother. To make the point, I wore his goggles propped up in my fiery hair throughout the school day until some teacher told me to take them off. And if I felt like it, I'd give certain of my classmates a ride. By sophomore year, they were almost always boys.

You wouldn't call me popular exactly, but I was hard to miss. I lived with crazy people and changed my own oil, and I was to be the first girl to bob her hair because I didn't have a mother to stop me.

I could draw quite a crowd of boys on a cold winter's afternoon when to get The Peewee started, I'd have to twist out the spark plugs and pour raw gasoline in the cylinders, and blow down the fuel tank.

They wouldn't let me take Auto Mechanics, but the rumor went round that I knew more than the teacher. I was better than average in math, and I took Latin, which got the kinks out of my grammar, as you see. And I got better and better at being myself because who wants to be everybody else?

I lived for the weekends Jake came back from Indianapolis, in a Stutz of his own. We'd move back into our homeplace and eat our suppers at the same kitchen table, with the old light coming through the window, though you can't turn back the clock. But Jake was there.

Then one weekend Jake came home in an army uniform with a Sam Brown belt, and puttees wrapped up his legs. Oh, he looked handsome in it, though blurry. I knew he'd sign up before they came for him. It was only a question of time.

We were in the war by then, the Great War, we called it, until a greater one, more awful, came later. It was the spring of my junior year, but I felt like a kid again. That lost.

"Are you and Grace going to—"

"Not till it's over," Jake said.

Meaning if he lived through it.

He left his Stutz with me to look after, and did I ever. I

kept it showroom fresh and never drove it to school, though it was asking to be shown off. I told myself I didn't want to put any miles on it. But in my heart I thought that if I kept it perfect, Jake would come back.

Time hung heavy after he'd shipped out, and I marveled at how long it was taking me to grow up. Then who turned up in a uniform next, but Irene. It was late spring and summer-hot, just evening, when she came up on the Hazelriggs' porch.

I saw her framed in the screen door, like a portrait of herself. I didn't know what her uniform signified. But, oh, she looked good in it, elegant and severe. She didn't need her spectacles now. And the uniform hat was perfect on her.

Once more, just in that single moment, I wanted to be her.

She'd joined the American Ambulance Field Service and was going for training to drive Stutz-built ambulances in France, leaving Geraldine and Lodelia to run the library. Another piece of my world broke off and fell away.

We strolled arm in arm down to the arbor, where the old table and chairs still stood, overgrown with vines. This year the grapes would make.

She'd come to say her good-byes. But after she'd admired my bob, a silence fell between us. "Eleanor," she said in her precise way, "something's weighing on my conscience."

I'd never seen her uncertain. It was a sight.

"In a way, it's about the Kirbys." Her tone was hushed.

The Kirbys? What in the—

"Well, not really about them," she said. "But I suppose all this time you've blamed them."

I stared at her through the leafy gloaming.

"Well, yes, if I have to think about them at all," I said, "I blame them. They burgled us blind for years. They sugared Grace's gas feed and cut her brake cable. They set fire to our dog. Growler brained Jake with a wrench. They burned down the garage. And to beat all, on the night before the race they stole our auto."

"No," Irene said in no more than a whisper. "They didn't steal your auto. Grace stole it. And I helped."

I stared. I couldn't grasp it. "You? Grace? No."

"We did," she said. "We broke in, pushed it outside, and tied it to the back of the Stoddard-Dayton. I've never been so frightened since. We hid it in the Muehlbach barn."

So that's why it had smelled like pigs, and still did, a little.

"We paid Mr. Muehlbach to store it and then to return it the next night. And we paid him a little extra. Hush money, I believe it's called. Grace did. But I'm guilty. I was an accessory."

I couldn't believe my ears. "Why, Irene?"

She looked aside at grape leaves. "You know what a determined girl Grace is. And an excellent planner. I don't know what we'd have done in the library without her excellent pl—"

"Get right to the point, Irene."

"She was determined that Jake win the race. She knew he couldn't win in the auto he'd built. But he could win in the Bearcat, and it would make him look good in her father's eyes. And his own, of course. She had his best interests at heart."

"And her own," I said.

"And her own," Irene said.

That far-off time came flooding back. The terrible, airless morning when we found The Peewee missing. Then purely by chance, Grace turned up to offer Jake the Bearcat. Of course, I'd won the race in place of Jake, but no plan's perfect.

"Does Jake know?" I inquired.

"No, and he never will unless you . . ."

Irene awaited my verdict. I let her wait awhile. Then I said, "Any girl who'd go to all that trouble to get him deserves to have him."

Irene almost sagged, relief written all over her. "Oh thank heaven," she said. "If I were to be killed in the war with this on my conscience, I could never live with myself."

A rare moment of confused thinking on her part.

Word of the war reached the Colonel. He sat through long evenings on the porch or before the stove, polishing his old boots and mess kit, waiting for a draft that would call up eighty-two-year-olds. He was still waiting the spring after the war was over, my senior year.

I didn't expect a graduation present from Aunt Hat. Why should I? They'd given me shelter and themselves, all the eggs I could eat and good home baking. And the company of a cat with a wooden paw. Who could ask for more? But on the night I graduated, she had something for me to see.

Taking me in hand, she led me up to the far end of the attic. I can see her seamed old black-walnut hands yet, working through all the debris to get to a dented army trunk. It was wedged where the roof met the floor in a scattering of mouse parts the cat hadn't eaten. She rummaged all through the trunk and finally found what she wanted to show me.

She held it up by lamplight, faded blue unfolding. It was the Colonel's Civil War uniform, heady with mothballs and old skirmishes. I took it in my hands, feeling where it had been, rejoicing that my brother was home and whole and would never wear a uniform again because his had been the War to End All Wars.

Aunt Hat watched me with that squint of hers. She waited with all her patience until I found the insignia on the sleeve of the Colonel's coat.

The sergeant's stripes.

But—

The Colonel had been a sergeant. He'd only been a colonel later, in his mind, and ours. And Aunt Hat let it be. She'd kept his secret all these years, and then gave it to me for graduation.

She was a woman of few words. Still, to complete my education, I suppose she wanted to make sure I knew what love is, before I went out into the world.

But of course I knew. I loved my brother, and home. And the sound of an engine turning over like a human heart and gunning smooth as song. And hot Hoosier summer mornings and the linger of firefly evenings. And the view over the hedgerows from the crown of the road.

On one of the days I'd been listening at high school, I heard about a young woman named Alice Ramsay who'd driven coast to coast across the American continent in an automobile, all on her own. And where there were roads, she used them, and when there was only open country, she lit out across it.

And it struck me that this was just exactly the way I wanted to live my whole life. So I went into the world, my brother's goggles slung around my neck in case the track got muddy.

CHAPTER FIFTEEN

INDY 500
1978

From the Indianapolis *World of Sport*, May 29, 1978:

The world's most famous auto race, the Indianapolis 500, roared through its sixty-second season today with the fastest thirty-three-car field in its history.

The winner, Mr. Al Unser, driving a turbocharged Lola-Cosworth, raised three fingers on Victory Lane to indicate this, his third Indy win, before quaffing the traditional glass of milk.

Some of his thunder was stolen, however, by Miss Janet Guthrie. She broke the 500's sex barrier in last year's race, but withdrew with mechanical difficulties. Boos and catcalls greeted her first Indy attempt, but this year she was cheered at every pit stop as she brought her Lightning-Offenhauser-powered car in to a ninth-place finish.

The race began with the stir-
ring command, "Lady and
Gentlemen, start your engines,"
broadcast in a ringing tone by
Mrs. Jake McGrath, the former
Grace Stutz of the legendary
Indianapolis automotive family.

In conferring the silver loving
cup on Mr. Unser, Grace Stutz
McGrath noted Janet Guthrie's
groundbreaking achievement. She
then pointed out her sister-in-law,
Miss Eleanor McGrath, a perky,
elderly figure peering down from a
seat in the Stutz box.

Fans of racing lore and
Hoosier history may just recall
Miss Eleanor McGrath. An ances-
tress of a sort to Miss Guthrie, she
was the only finisher in the first
Hendricks County fair dirt-track
event in the distant year of 1914.
Her achievement was all the more
impressive for her extreme youth
and sex and the rough-and-ready
lawlessness of Indiana's early auto
racing days.

As she spans the history of automobile racing, this newspaper
asked the venerable Miss McGrath
how racing had changed.

"Well, the purse is a good deal
better now. Right at a million,
two? It was fifty dollars in my race,
and they robbed me of it." Miss
McGrath sniffed and added, "Men."

And how did she find Miss Janet Guthrie as a driver?

"Looked to me like she drove a good, conservative race, with her turbocharger booster turned down to conserve fuel in the first couple hundred miles. Andretti and Foyt got past her, but she moved up fine for the finish." Miss McGrath peered sharply through her bifocals, adding, "But what would I know? I finished backwards."

Then she settled back in her box seat beside the elegant Mrs. Grace McGrath, their two snow-white heads close amid the snapping checkered flag of Gasoline Alley and the Victory Lane.

Literature Circle Questions

Use these questions and the activities that follow to get more out of the experience of reading *Here Lies the Librarian* by Richard Peck.

1. Sparks's tail is nearly burned off in chapter 9, but there is something even stranger about Aunt Hat and Colonel Hazelrigg's pet. What is unusual about their pet?

2. Irene Ridpath turns "whiter than chalk" in chapter 2 when she discovers something unexpected about Peewee. Name what she learns and three other things that surprise Irene about life outside the big city of Indianapolis.

3. List four unexpected things that occur during the ten-mile Hendricks County auto race.

4. Explain several ways the four prospective librarians represent the "bargain of the century."

5. Create a Venn diagram that shows the differences and similarities between Jake McGrath, Peewee McGrath, and Grace Stutz.

6. Eleanor believes Jake and Irene are sweet on each other, but the author gives us clues that suggest it is actually Jake and Grace who get along the best. What is the turning point in Jake's relationship with Grace?

7. Imagine that you a reporter for the Indianapolis *Star* in 1914 and are writing an article on the car business. Write five interview questions to ask various people in the novel. You may direct your questions to anyone you like.

8. What might have happened if Jake's homemade auto hadn't been stolen the night before the Hendricks County auto race?

9. Even though Eleanor is brave enough to spend a night in jail, stand up to the Kirbys, and race a car, she is gripped with fear when asked to pour punch at the library tea in chapter 7. Compare this contradiction in Eleanor's behavior with something in your own personality.

10. In chapter 12, after Jake's car accident, Irene surprises Eleanor by saying, "Who'd want to be on the pit crew when you could be in the race?" Why do you think Irene says this?

11. Create an acrostic for one of the characters in the novel.

12. Choose one of the characters and plan a party for him or her. Your party should have a theme, a guest speaker, decorations, games, refreshments, and anything else you can think of to make it a special event. Write a short toast in honor of your chosen character.

13. How do you suppose Eleanor would have used the $50 in prize money from the auto race?

14. Despite Irene's attempts to persuade her, Eleanor does not attend Irene's alma mater, "the best girls' school in Indianapolis," but stays in her own hometown. Did Eleanor make the right decision? Justify your answer.

15. It seems that neither Irene nor Eleanor has ever encountered someone quite like the other. Who do you think learned the most from their relationship?

Note: These questions are keyed to Bloom's Taxonomy as follows: Knowledge: 1-3; Comprehension: 4-6; Application: 7-8; Analysis: 9-10; Synthesis: 11-12; Evaluation: 13-15.

Activities

1. Electra Dietz's tombstone inscription is uniquely connected to her career as town librarian. Create a headstone that carries a similar significance for another character in *Here Lies the Librarian*. In addition to a creative epitaph and headstone decoration, be sure to include the character's name and birth and death dates. Base all details on what you've learned from the book. For instance, we know Irene is 19 years old when the book begins in 1914, so if Irene had already celebrated her birthday, she must have been born in 1895. The Colonel's passion for his efforts during the Civil War might inspire you to add a Union flag to his tombstone.

2. Author Richard Peck uses several words that are no longer common today. For instance, Mrs. B. D. Klinefelder's "step-ins" (chapter 2) are strewn about by the tornado, and Jake and Peewee's garage started life as a "livery stable" (chapter 1). Create a glossary explaining 15 words that you learned in this novel. Create illustrations of your own for three of these words.

3. Write a newspaper article about one of the characters from *Here Lies the Librarian*, dated five years after the end of chapter 14. Your article can be from any section of the newspaper — the crime blotter, the fashion or sports pages, the business section, or even the obituaries. Be sure to include a catchy headline and quotes. Reread the newspaper articles that Richard Peck wrote for this book to inspire you as you write your article.

Also by Richard Peck

The Teacher's Funeral: A Comedy in Three Parts, companion novel to *Here Lies the Librarian*